2nd in
Insp Madoc Rhys (RCMP)
Series

MURDER GOES MUMMING

By Alisa Craig

MURDER GOES MUMMING
THE GRUB-AND-STAKERS MOVE A MOUNTAIN
A PINT OF MURDER

MURDER GOES MUMMING

ALISA CRAIG

DOUBLEDAY & COMPANY, INC.
GARDEN CITY, NEW YORK

All of the characters in this book
are fictitious, and any resemblance
to actual persons, living or dead,
is purely coincidental.

ISBN 0-385-17887-5

For Ailsa, Anita, and Phyllis

The author is indebted to Stuart Trueman for information about the Phantom Ship of Bay Chaleur, to Chief M. T. Quigley of the Dalhousie Police Department for his kind assistance, and to A. Martin Winchester for his helpful comments.

MURDER GOES MUMMING

CHAPTER 1

Detective Inspector Madoc Rhys was a happy man. He had a four-day Christmas holiday by official ukase from RCMP Headquarters at Fredericton, New Brunswick, and he was about to take Miss Janet Wadman to dinner.

Rhys had been seeing a good deal of Miss Janet Wadman since she'd returned to her job in Saint John this past September, though not so much as he would have wished. The nature of his own profession tended to require his presence at the scenes of mysterious malefactions whose perpetrators never bothered to consider that it would have been kind of them to commit their crimes closer to Miss Wadman's temporary abode.

Janet was lodging in a furnished room with a widow lady of high principles and suspicious nature. Madoc Rhys had been allowed into that room for the first time this same afternoon, and then only because he'd brought his mother with him. He smiled at the memory as he adjusted his tie.

He'd phoned down from Fredericton and told Janet he was coming to meet his mother who was on her way to join his father in London. Being Janet she'd replied, "I can't ask her to supper in this room, because I have nowhere to cook it, but if you'd like to. bring her for a cup of tea, she's welcome. I do have an electric kettle."

Madoc's mother was not used to being entertained in bed-sitters by farmers' daughters working as stenographers. She'd been a trifle starchy at first, but Janet's scones and lemon cheese tarts had soon thawed her out. When she'd exclaimed,

"I do so wish we had a bakery like yours at home," Janet had turned bright pink and primmed her lips.

Madoc, being a truly astute detective, had at once realized why. "What did you do, Jenny?" he'd asked. "Get up at five o'clock and swipe your landlady's oven?"

"Well, you can't serve boughten pastry to a person's *mother*," she'd replied.

Moments later, Janet had addressed that mother as Mrs. Rhys and had to be told that Mrs. Rhys was in fact Lady Rhys, wife of Sir Emlyn Rhys the noted choral director, mother of Dafydd Rhys the famous operatic tenor, and of Gwendolyn Rhys the rising young clarinetist. Furthermore, Lady Rhys herself had once sung "Ah, sweet mystery of life at last I've found thee" in front of the Queen Mum before she'd sacrificed her own musical career to those of her distinguished husband and her gifted children, and for goodness' sake hadn't Madoc *explained*?

Far from being overawed, Janet had observed wasn't that just like Madoc and offered Lady Rhys another lemon cheese tart for the road. On the way back to their hotel, Lady Rhys, who had always found her renegade second son a sore trial, had remarked that the Wadmans must be a very decent family and thank heaven Madoc had shaved off that God-awful moustache.

Without the drooping, reddish fringe on his upper lip, Detective Inspector Rhys looked less like an out-of-work plumber's helper and more like an aspiring young poet whose parents had a little money. He'd got his wavy, almost black hair cut by a barber who was not a lineal descendant of Sweeney Todd, bought some decent clothes for a change, and begun having a different sort of trouble with his female suspects than he was accustomed to.

Tonight Madoc was wearing the dinner jacket he'd acquired as a hand-me-down from Dafydd when he was eighteen because his mother insisted one never knew whom one was going to meet and one owed it to one's father's position. Lady Rhys had tactfully given Janet to understand that a dinner gown was not absolutely *de rigueur*. Janet had been astonished that anybody could even think she owned a formal gown, much less would wear it out in public unless to a Grand Installation of the Loyal Order of Owls or some such overwhelmingly solemn event. She did have a long red velvet skirt she'd bought because it was warmer around the legs than a short one. Lady Rhys said the skirt sounded perfect. Madoc thought it sounded rather dressy for a Saint John restaurant but had sense enough not to say so, knowing he himself was stuck with Dafydd's old suit in any case and not wanting to upset the applecart, which was trundling along so delightfully. Besides, he wanted to see how Janet looked in red velvet.

Janet was no longer the hagridden, desperately courageous little creature Rhys had met last August and managed to keep from becoming corpse number three in one of the most bizarre cases of multiple murder he'd ever handled.* He hadn't quite realized how much she'd changed until he'd seen her beside his own mother this afternoon, quite at ease and blooming like an out-of-season rose.

He took a taxi to the rooming house and recklessly kept it waiting while his adored one put on the finishing touches and came down. Janet's landlady, who had been wont to eye Rhys as a potential seducer and betrayer and hadn't put any real stock in that yarn about his mother's coming to tea, was sufficiently awed by the splendor of Dafydd's old suit to attempt a smile and hope Mr. Rhys's mother was enjoying her visit to Saint John.

"I'm sorry I didn't get to meet her," she added rather pointedly.

"Yes, well, I'm sure Mother would have enjoyed meeting you, too," Rhys answered because his profession required him

* *A Pint of Murder,* Doubleday Crime Club, 1980.

to do a considerable amount of lying anyway and it was, after all, the season to be jolly. "Ah, there you are, Jenny. Right on the button."

"I didn't want to keep Lady Rhys waiting."

Janet gave her now open-mouthed landlady a pleasant nod as she swept out of the house in her skirt and the beaver cape her sister-in-law Annabelle had insisted on lending her because Annabelle was no fool and had seen which way the wind was blowing as soon as Janet had started bringing Madoc up to the farm for weekends. The cape had in fact belonged to Annabelle's grandmother but was well preserved because the Duprees always bought quality and took good care of it. An attached hood and a fat little barrel muff completed as captivating a costume as was ever flaunted before an infatuated male.

"You're straight off a Christmas card," said Madoc, helping himself to an extra kiss as he put her into the taxi. "I suppose you realize Mother's crazy about you. While we're on the subject, so am I."

"I'd begun to have a feeling you might be." Janet snuggled up close and let the hood fall so that her soft bronze-brown hair rested against his cheek. "That makes it cozy all around."

Unfortunately, they had only a short ride to the hotel. Lady Rhys was waiting for them in the lobby, doing Sir Emlyn proud in black velvet and diamonds. She was chatting with some Very Important Person whose name she couldn't recall.

"My son Madoc and his fiancée, Janet Wadman," she introduced airily.

The Very Important Person observed in all sincerity that Madoc was a fortunate young man and took his departure. Madoc protested, though with no great violence.

"Mother, Janet hasn't said she'd marry me yet."

"Madoc, don't be silly. You two are obviously besotted with each other and Janet is hardly the sort to go in for anything silly like those young nitwits Dafydd is always hopping in and out of bed with. I've got to leave Saint John airport on the stroke of midnight to connect with my overseas flight from Halifax, and I have no time to waste on pussyfooting."

Lady Rhys took off a relatively modest but still impressive diamond. "This was my own grandmother's engagement ring. I decided long ago that I'd pass it on to whichever of my children got married first. Janet, I should be greatly honored if you'd let Madoc give it to you now."

Janet started to say, "Oh, I couldn't't," then caught Madoc's eye, which was both besotted and beseeching, and decided she might as well. Shortly thereafter she shed her cape and muff, fixed her hair, which had got disarranged from all the kissing and hugging, and swept into the dining room between her betrothed and the distinguished lady who was so determined to be her mother-in-law. She looked so radiant in her red velvet skirt and little red vest with a white ruffled shirtwaist under it that any number of diners turned to stare and Madoc nearly exploded with pride.

He ordered champagne, expressing the courteous hope that the bubbles wouldn't get up Janet's nose and make her sneeze the way his moustache had done the first time he kissed her. Janet blushed an even more dazzling shade of rose and told him that was a fine way to talk in front of his mother. Lady Rhys wondered if perhaps they shouldn't have the wedding at St. Gregory's. Janet replied politely but firmly that the wedding would be held in the Pitcherville Reformed Baptist Church and that her brother Bert would give her away.

"In his Loyal Order of Owls regalia?" Madoc teased.

"If it makes him happy," she replied. "And we'd be delighted to have you sing 'Ah, Sweet Mystery of Life,' Lady Rhys, if you will. We're all very fond of the Queen Mum back home."

That struck Lady Rhys as hilarious. She laughed until she had to blot away the tears with her napkin because she owed it to her husband's position to present a decorous countenance before his great Canadian public.

"I haven't had so much fun in ages. I do wish I could take darling Jenny to London with me. She'd take the starch out of a few stuffed shirts. By the way, Madoc, what are you two planning to do for Christmas?"

"Oh, I thought we might just sit on a bench in King Square and hold hands," her son replied. "Actually I haven't had time to think about it much. Do you want to go up to Pitcherville, Jenny?"

"Not particularly. Annabelle's brother and his tribe are coming down from Rivière-du-Loup and her folks will be up, too. The house will be popping at the seams. I don't know where they'd put us, unless we bunk over at the Mansion with Marion Emery."

"Scratch Pitcherville, then."

Rhys had been forced to spend a couple of nights at the Mansion when he'd first gone there on official business and had no desire to take further advantage of Marion's hospitality. "Perhaps I'll keep my room here at the hotel and we can see a couple of movies or something. Your landlady might even let me come up for another cup of tea, now that we're on the verge of making it legal."

He was trying to kiss the back of Janet's neck, and she was telling him to behave himself when another Very Important Person stopped at their table.

"Here's a merry party. How nice to see you again, Lady Rhys. What brings you to Saint John?"

"Mr. Condrycke, what a pleasant surprise! Won't you join us for a glass of champagne to celebrate my son Madoc's engagement? This is my new daughter-in-law to be, Janet Wadman. Isn't she lovely?"

"She is, indeed. Congratulations, Rhys. Miss Wadman," he looked a trifle puzzled as he took the hand she held out to him. "Is it possible we've met somewhere?"

"Not to say met," Janet replied. "I was the one who took in the tea at your board meeting day before yesterday when

Miss Perse was laid up with flu. You were the only one who bothered to say thank you."

"Well, well!"

Mr. Condrycke threw back his handsome blond-gray head and laughed. "That goes to show politeness always pays. One never knows whom one's going to meet where these days. So you're another of those liberated ladies who go in for careers? You must meet my daughter. Valerie's determined to break into television, don't ask me why. And you're a musician, I suppose, like the rest of your distinguished family. Eh, Rhys?"

"No, I'm the black sheep," Madoc admitted. "I was born with a tin ear."

"Madoc works for the Canadian government. In research."

Lady Rhys glared at her son, daring him to say her nay. He had no wish to do so, not because he wasn't proud to be a Mountie but because he often found it prudent not to advertise the fact.

"Computers and that sort of thing, I suppose," Mr. Condrycke said not very interestedly. He took the chair Lady Rhys indicated and the glass the waiter filled for him. "To your very good health and happiness, Mr. and Mrs. Rhys. And a Merry Christmas to all. What are your plans for the holidays?"

"We were just talking about that," said Lady Rhys. "I'm off to London tonight to meet my husband. He's doing the *Messiah* for the Royal Family. Dafydd's singing the tenor and our daughter Gwendolyn will be in the orchestra so it's quite a family affair, except for Madoc. He claimed he couldn't get the time off to join us and now I understand why."

She gave Janet an indulgent smile. "It's a pity these two couldn't have got their plans together a bit sooner. Janet's people are having a big house party and don't have room for them, so it looks as if they'll be all by themselves right here in Saint John. Can you imagine anything more deadly?"

She was joking, of course, but Mr. Condrycke seemed to think she wasn't. "That's terrible! Can't be allowed. Excuse me one moment, I'm going to get my wife."

"Who's this Mr. Condrycke?" Madoc asked as the man left the table.

"He's a patron of the arts," Lady Rhys replied rather grandly. "One meets them at benefits and receptions. I believe Dafydd took the daughter out once or twice when he came here to sing in a Community Concert."

"That is quite possible," said Rhys. "There are not many families whose daughters Dafydd has not taken out. Or in, as the case may be."

"Really, Madoc! What will Jenny think?"

"I hope she'll think she was lucky to meet me instead of Dafydd, though that is a great deal to hope. Jenny love, what do you know about Mr. Condrycke?"

"He's the one member of the board everybody seems to like, is all I can tell you. His first name is Donald, not that I've ever got to use it, needless to say. He's not around the offices much, and I've never had any personal contact with him except that one time with the tea. We've been short-handed these past few days. You know how people tend to come down with mysterious ailments around the holidays. Anyway, Mr. Condrycke speaks to people in elevators and that sort of thing, and always looks good-natured, which makes him conspicuous among the top brass."

"Has he been with the company long?"

"Forever, I believe, though I haven't been there long enough myself to say for sure. It's my impression the Condryckes were among the founding fathers."

"I shouldn't be surprised," said Lady Rhys. "He looks like old money."

"Mother, what a snob you are," cried Madoc.

"No, dear, just aware of who's good for a decent-sized donation and who isn't. Music is so often a grace and favor sort of business, you know. Do stop detecting and try to act like a gentleman for once. Ask that waiter to bring us another chair for Mrs. Condrycke, and another bottle of bubbly."

"I shall need a decent-sized donation to pay for this meal if you insist on turning it into a formal reception."

"Nonsense, Madoc. You know Aunt Oldrys Rhys-Brown left you pots of money."

"Not pots, Mother."

"Well, a good deal more than she left the rest of us. Aunt Oldrys always hated music. I strongly suggest you two find yourselves a decent house straightaway instead of going into lodgings. Jenny will be leading much the same sort of life I've had to, I expect, either trailing around after you to heaven knows where or else at home with the babies wondering whether your plane's crashed or your lead soprano's having a temperament. Though with you I expect it will be bullets and burglars. In any event, she must have a place of her own. There's always so much bother about a house that it keeps one's mind off what one's husband may have got himself into when one's not around to look after him. Mrs. Condrycke, how very nice to see you again. Are we taking you away from a party?"

"Yes, but it's a company affair and quite frankly I'm delighted at the excuse to slip away. You see, Miss Wadman, I'm throwing myself on your mercy not to repeat that. Donald tells me you're a member of the firm, too. Though soon to become an ex-member?"

Mrs. Condrycke's manner was just gracious enough, her smile just the right degree arch as she glanced with proper respect at the fine heirloom diamond gracing Janet's left hand.

"I hardly qualify as a member of the firm," Janet replied with, Madoc was amused to note, the perfect mixture of modesty and amusement. "And I expect I shall be leaving before I've managed to scrabble my way out of the stenographic pool."

"Shall you miss it, do you think?"

"With all respect to the firm, not a bit. I like keeping house, and I think office work is a bore."

"Then you must have a heart-to-heart chat with my daughter Val. Which brings us, as that other bore who's making the speech back there is probably saying about now, to the true object of our meeting. My husband and I are hoping we can persuade you and Madoc to come up to Graylings with us."

"Graylings is up on the Bay Chaleur, not too far from Dalhousie," Mr. Condrycke explained. "My father and some other members of our family live there year round. We're a bit feudal in our ways, and we tend to go all out for Christmas. Yule logs and wassail bowls and silly jokes, you know. It's totally informal and great fun. At least we think so. Don't we, Babs?"

His wife nodded. "The Condryckes are the jolliest crowd imaginable and the house is a gem. Enormous and about a hundred years behind the times, but quite comfortable, really. Squire—that's our pet name for my father-in-law—even has an old retainer who brings one morning tea in the real old English tradition. It's like taking a step backward in time. Huge open fires and, thank goodness, a hot-air furnace of sorts and some airtight stoves to put back the heat the fires suck up the chimneys. And tons of lovely food. I always have to put Donald on a diet after we've been to Graylings."

"She does, indeed," laughed Donald Condrycke. "Valerie's bringing her current young man and my nephews will be home from boarding school; so you kids can enjoy watching us oldsters make fools of ourselves. Please say you'll come."

It was hard to picture the Condryckes making fools of themselves, but quite possible to believe Graylings would be an agreeable place to spend the holiday. Janet, who'd never been much of anywhere, was trying to look poised and gracious, and in fact giving a pretty good imitation of Cinderella being presented with a brand-new pumpkin. Lady Rhys was clearly pleased with herself, her hand-picked daughter-in-law and even, as a startling change from custom, with her son. Having chosen such a different path from the rest of his family, Madoc hadn't thought about what Janet might encounter when she was with her future in-laws. Perhaps he ought to let her have this taste of what being a Rhys could mean.

"Thank you," he replied. "If you're quite sure you want us, Janet and I will be delighted to come up for a day or two. Won't we Jenny?"

"It's kind of you to ask us," Janet said in the sweet, low voice that was going to delight Sir Emlyn when he got to hear it. "What shall we bring?"

CHAPTER 2

The Condryckes offered a ride up to Graylings in their car, but Madoc was loath to give up a day alone with his Jenny. "Just tell us where it is and we'll find the place."

"It's a long drive," Babs Condrycke replied doubtfully, "and we'd hate you to miss dinner. Isn't it tomorrow night we do the Yule log, Donald?"

"Half past six on the dot. Then the wassail and the roast goose. I hope you eat goose, Miss Wadman."

"I generally eat what's put in front of me," she replied in the prim Pitcherville way Madoc found so adorable. "We'll be there on time if Madoc says we can. Now shouldn't we be thinking about getting Lady Rhys to the airport?"

They said their farewells to their prospective host and hostess, and set about getting Madoc's mother out of her diamonds and into her traveling costume. While she was changing, Janet and Madoc telephoned up to Pitcherville. Annabelle was smug when Janet said she'd been wearing the beaver cape when Madoc put the ring on her finger and flabbergasted when she learned what sort of family Janet would be marrying into. Bert got on the phone amid great babble from the background and hoped his sister wouldn't be too high and mighty to speak to her poor relations. Madoc said she damn well wouldn't and Bert had better get set to catch him when he fainted at the wedding, and here was Mother to say hello.

Thereupon, Lady Rhys said hello and a great deal more about how delighted she was that Madoc had found such a wonderful girl and what a credit Janet was to her upbringing, which of course was a most delicate compliment to Bert and Annabelle, who'd raised his younger sister since she'd been orphaned while still at school. At last they hung up in an atmosphere of long-distance bonhomie and went to the airport. The long taxi ride back was the best part of all.

The next morning Janet was up betimes and, while she waited for Madoc to take her to breakfast, regaled her awestruck landlady with an account of how Lady Rhys had sung for the Queen Mum.

They spent a long time over the meal, trying to have a serious discussion about the things they ought to be seriously considering and having to break off to say the things they really wanted to say. After that, Madoc took Janet to Birks.

"I meant for us to pick out the ring today," he explained. "Do you really like that one Mother gave us, or would you rather have something different? You'll be wearing it for the rest of your life, you know."

"I know."

Janet gave him such a misty-eyed smile he was forced to kiss her right there on the sidewalk, to the delight of many Christmas shoppers and the Salvation Army lassie who was collecting donations on the corner.

"I adore the ring, darling, and I wouldn't dream of hurting your mother's feelings by choosing another in its place. Why don't you just buy me a nice, plain one to go with it?"

So they picked out a wedding ring for Janet but not for Madoc because wedding rings were noticeable and in his line of work it was often better not to be. Then Madoc wanted to buy Janet some diamond earrings to go with her engagement ring, but she talked him into a string of pearls that would be modest enough for Pitcherville but elegant enough to wear before royalty should she ever have occasion, as it now seemed entirely possible she might.

They then returned to get Madoc's luggage and check him out of the hotel, retrieve his car from the garage, and swing around to collect Janet's suitcase from her now totally overwhelmed landlady. At that point Janet gave Madoc the russet wool sweater she'd spent all fall knitting him because she couldn't stand to wait till Christmas Day and he might as well have it to wear up at the Condryckes' because goodness knew what the weather would be like up there. She herself wasn't banking any too heavily on that old hot-air furnace and had packed her thermal underwear just in case.

Then Madoc had to try on the sweater, which fitted him perfectly and made him look far handsomer than the pictures Lady Rhys had shown Janet of his famous brother Dafydd. What with one thing and another, they were impossibly late starting what would have been roughly a three-hundred-mile drive, so they drove the sixty-five miles to Fredericton, dropped in at RCMP Headquarters to receive general felicitations as well as sandwiches and mugs of tea gratis from the canteen, got rid of Madoc's car, and bummed a lift in a helicopter that happened to be headed up Dalhousie way.

The pilot knew Graylings even without Madoc's directions. According to him, the place wasn't all that close to Dalhousie but 'way the hell and gone out in the middle of nowhere. He was surprised Madoc and Janet had got invited. The Condryckes were a clannish lot, though he guessed they did throw the odd bash for visiting swells when the mood was upon them.

"Big place, I understand," Madoc observed.

"Cripes, I'll say. Looks from the air like one of those old castles or something."

"Costs a packet to keep up, eh?"

"Oh, I doubt there's any dearth of money in that crowd. You warm enough, Janet? There's hot tea in the Thermos behind you, and an extra blanket if you need it."

"Thanks. Right now I'm so excited I couldn't tell you whether I'm cold or not. I've never been up in one of these things before."

"Besides, she's got her thermal underwear," Madoc added, reaching from the seat behind to tuck Janet up in the blanket and get in a squeeze or two. Even in ski pants and a down jacket, Janet was an eminently huggable young woman.

They had their tea. After a while, Janet began to weary of white snow and green-black forest and the noise of rotor blades overhead. The sky grayed, then darkened. It was an ineffable relief when the pilot shouted at last, "We're going down," and brought his craft's skis to rest on a vast plowed-out driveway in front of the biggest private dwelling she'd ever been this close to.

By now it was really dark, a beautiful clear night with each separate star glittering like the diamond in her new engagement ring. As she climbed stiffly out of the helicopter, Janet could feel tiny icicles forming inside her nose.

"Thank you again for the ride," she called up to the pilot. "You come and see us as soon as we have a house."

"Don't forget your thermal underwear. You'll want it up here, that's for sure."

He handed down the bags. Janet and Madoc walked up the steps of Graylings and thumped on the knocker.

A tall, handsome, elderly replica of Donald answered the door. This must be Squire himself. He was all affability.

"Here you are, just in time. Delighted you could come. Good God, what's that racket? Donald, Babs, they've flown up in a helicopter. Come and see, quick!"

A great many large blond people crowded to the front windows to watch the flying bug take off. They all appeared to think young Rhys and his bride-to-be had done something screamingly funny by arriving in this really not so unusual way. For a country as big and as underpopulated as Canada, small aircraft were often the most practical form of transport.

Anyway, it was pleasant to find themselves getting off on the right foot among so merry a party. Mrs. Condrycke came forward to do her part as hostess. She was wearing an ankle-length skirt of handwoven wool in the Black Watch tartan and a dark green mohair pullover with a rolled neck, managing to look chic and warm at the same time. Her only ornaments, Janet was pleased to note, were her diamond rings and a nice string of pearls.

"Do call me Babs," she urged. "The only Mrs. Condrycke around here is Granny, who hasn't come downstairs yet. My husband is Donald, as you doubtless know. Squire is Squire and he gets livid if you call him anything else. Don't you, Squire darling?"

"Positively foam at the mouth," he agreed. "We must get these young adventurers into something comfortable right away. You must be half-frozen, Miss Wadman. Or may I say Janet?"

"Please say Janet."

She couldn't picture Squire foaming at the mouth, except perchance over a tankard of brown October ale. He looked like the embodiment of all the Squire Allworthys who'd ever galloped across a British countryside. He even had on suitably ancient plus fours and knitted wool socks in a brown and yellow argyle pattern, with a bright yellow pullover and a tweed jacket with suede leather patches at the elbows. Like the other Condryckes he was tall and burly and fair, with eyes of a clear light blue.

In fact, the entire group looked much alike. Babs was another blue-eyed blond, and so were the rest of the in-laws. A family that came in matched sets was going to be a problem to keep sorted out. Janet tried to remember some of the professional tricks Madoc had taught her about remembering people's faces as they thronged around clamoring for introductions.

The woman who was even taller and somewhat older than Babs, and who looked the most like Squire, was his eldest daughter May, who appeared to function as housekeeper at Graylings. Like Babs, May had on a long skirt and sweater, but her skirt was checked in a dazzle of red, green, and yellow. Her pullover was the same canary yellow as her father's. Around her neck hung a gold pendant made to represent a parrot and enameled in the same vivid shades as her skirt. The thing was about the size of a real chickadee and when she pulled the tail it flapped its wings and squawked. Janet laughed more from surprise than amusement, and May roared with her.

"Isn't this priceless! Herbert gave me the bird for our last anniversary. He claims it reminds him of me. Don't you, you old louse?"

May put a neat hammer lock on a tall, blond, jovial soul who was running a bit to fat, and dragged him to the fore. "This is my ever-loving husband Herbert, who's Squire's steward when he can get his mind off other things. Don't let him back you into any dark corners, Janet. Ever-loving doesn't necessarily mean he's loving *me*."

"Pay no attention to my wife, Janet," drawled the alleged lady-killer. "I never do."

He gave May a mighty whack on the rump with his left hand and stretched out the right to shake hands.

Madoc managed to get his own hand in before Janet's and was not a whit surprised to feel a tingling buzz against his palm. May thought this was pretty funny, too.

"Didn't I tell you he was a louse? We've got a couple of sons around somewhere, as I dimly recall. They'll show up for dinner, no doubt. And this is my sister Clara. Shake hands like a good little girl, Clara."

"Not with Herbert, I won't. How nice to meet you, Janet. Madoc, we're so glad you could come. Do you sing like your brother? And don't you positively hate being asked?"

Clara was either several years younger than May or a good deal better preserved. Her skirt was a discreet blue and beige plaid with a faint wine-colored stripe, and she wore a light blue pullover with a string of garnets.

"I do not sing like my brother," Rhys assured Clara. "Nobody does. Not even my brother, sometimes."

That quip raised another laugh from one and all. Janet was

beginning to feel uncomfortably warm inside the ski suit she still had on, and to realize how tired she was. She managed to get through a couple more introductions, not sure which was Clara's husband Lawrence the lawyer and which was Clara's brother Cyril. There didn't seem to be any Mrs. Cyril.

"Now we really must let these two get changed," Squire intervened with a slight edge to his geniality. "They'll meet the rest at dinner. It's after six already and we've still the Yule log to do. Get along, May, show them upstairs."

"I'll do it," Babs volunteered. "Where are you putting them, May?"

"Janet will have to share with Val, since Val towed that devastatingly unforgettable young what's-his-name along and didn't tell us in advance. I've given him the room that would otherwise have been Madoc's, and Madoc can have the one next door to Janet and Val, which Janet would have had if I hadn't given it to Madoc. Nicely confused, everyone? I'll buzz on out to the kitchen and see how Fifine's making out, and with whom. Herbert, you'd better drag the young fry out of the billiard room if that's where they are. Clara, would you mind checking the table?"

May stamped off, pulling her parrot's tail and laughing at the squawk as though she'd never heard it before. Madoc looked around for his and Janet's luggage.

"Oh, Ludovic will have taken up your bags. This way, please. Luckily we have electricity of sorts on the staircase and in the bathrooms when the dynamo's working. Oil lamps or candles elsewhere, I'm afraid. There's always talk of wiring all Graylings, but it never happens. Do mind the turns, they're tricky. Perhaps you haven't seen a switchback staircase before. I never knew such things existed till I married Donald. I'm still not quite sure they do."

Babs laughed as she led them up a dimly lighted, strangely zigzagging stairway that seemed to have at least one window and two landings to each flight. Madoc kept a protective arm around Janet so that she wouldn't be apt to stumble on one of the pie-shaped steps at the turns, which didn't make for the soundest of footing. Janet was glad of the support for several reasons, but mostly because it was Madoc's arm and not someone else's.

CHAPTER 3

"Janet, you're in here. We gave Val this big room when she was a youngster because she always liked to bring her girlfriends when we came. Now she brings her boyfriends, but we're creatures of habit. You're quite sure you won't mind sharing? That's a trundle bed underneath the fourposter. You just pull it out and flip a coin to see who gets which."

Babs demonstrated, making sure the trundle bed was properly made up. Janet was relieved to see there were good, thick Hudson Bay blankets on it.

"No, I don't mind sharing. I'm used to roommates."

Janet was relieved that she'd at least get a bed to herself, and it was only for a night or two anyway. She had a sneaking hunch Babs might be putting her into service as a chaperon, since there must surely be some other place she could camp in a house this size. On the other hand, perhaps Valerie was supposed to chaperon her. It was an amusing thought.

"Madoc, you're right next door. This used to be a boudoir and there's room enough in it to swing a cat if you don't pick too big a cat."

Babs laughed with what might almost have been a naughty imitation of May's lusty guffaw and opened a door connecting the two rooms. "You can lock this if you're feeling prudish. There, you see. What they call functional."

The room allotted to Rhys was in truth not much smaller than the bedroom Janet had slept in most of her life back at the farm, and far less simply furnished. Some antique dealer would give his eyeteeth for that roped cherrywood bedstead. It must date from Loyalist times, maybe even from the early

French settlers. Madoc was amused to see both his and Janet's bags on the luggage rack.

"Here, Jenny, this is yours." He carried it back into the larger room for her. "We shall be very comfortable, Babs. Are there really bathrooms?"

"Four, thank goodness, but they're all clustered in one place, around the main chimney just across the hall here. To keep the pipes from freezing, you see."

"Of course. An extremely sensible arrangement."

"Use any one that isn't occupied. There should be plenty of hot water and towels. And we have just about fifteen minutes before we light the Yule log, so please be as quick as you can. Put on whatever you're comfortable in. As you see, we don't dress."

Janet took the not dressing for what it was worth and decided she'd be most comfortable in her red velvet skirt. She wished she dared stretch out for a few minutes' rest on that cozy-looking trundle bed, but she did manage a quick hot shower, taking her clothes into the bathroom with her to steam out the travel creases as best she could. When she emerged in the long skirt, a lacy white cable knit pullover Mama Dupree had made for her last Christmas, and her new pearl necklace, she met Madoc, freshly shaven and damp about the ears, coming out of the bathroom next to hers.

"Integrating with the group, I see."

He smiled and pulled her close. "My darling Jenny, how beautiful you are. I hope you're going to enjoy this."

"I expect I'd enjoy anything so long as I had you with me," she murmured, rubbing her lips along his clean, warm jawbone. "Come on, we mustn't miss the Yule log, whatever that is. I've never seen one. Have you?"

"Oh, yes. At my great-uncle's place in Wales they always do it. We'll go there next Christmas, eh?"

"Let's cross that ocean when we come to it. All sorts of things can happen before then. What have you done with your shaving things?"

"Nagging already, are you?"

Madoc dutifully fetched his gear from the bathroom. Laughing, they ran hand-in-hand down the hall to their bedrooms. When Janet popped in to get rid of the clothes she'd worn in the helicopter and run a comb through her hair, she found yet another tall blond in designer blue jeans and a fabulous Icelandic sweater, doing things to her face at the dressing table mirror.

"Hello," she said. "You must be Valerie Condrycke. I'm Janet Wadman."

"Hi. Mum warned me I was getting a roommate." Valerie didn't sound altogether thrilled at meeting her. "She said you came up with Dafydd Rhys's brother. He never told me he had one."

"Well, Madoc isn't musical. There's a sister, too. They're in London right now with their parents."

"Why aren't you?"

"Madoc couldn't get away from his job long enough. Anyway, we only got engaged last night. He's waiting for me now so I'd better scoot. I'll see you downstairs, eh?"

Janet was not eager to be pumped about Madoc's family until she'd had a chance to glean some more information from him. She understood perfectly why he hadn't cared to make a parade of being Sir Emlyn's son. No doubt he'd run into any number of people who'd been ready to make up to him on the strength of his connections, as the Condryckes were doing now. Anyway, it wouldn't have mattered to her who he was, and it still didn't. Detective Inspector Madoc Rhys was the man she'd decided it would be awfully nice to be married to when she was frying his breakfast eggs last summer in Pitcherville, and Mrs. Madoc Rhys was who she was going to be and that was title enough for her. Nevertheless, she was not about to be patronized by any willowy snip with a Calvin Klein label plastered across her backside, even if she did take Valerie's father his tea in the conference room.

At that moment Madoc, bless his heart, rapped on the connecting door and called, "Jenny love, are you ready?"

"Coming." Janet poked her hair with the hand that wore the diamond so Val could see it flash in the lamplight, settled her pearls about her throat, and sailed out of the room head up and tail a-risin', as her father used to say. Sir Emlyn or no Sir Emlyn, she had a position of her own to consider.

The room downstairs they called the Great Hall since it was much too vast to be a parlor and too well-furnished for a ballroom, was now even fuller of Condryckes than it had been before. Two tall, skinny boys perhaps fifteen and seventeen years old were over by the door on the far side, with a thick rope slung over their shoulders. Squire was chivying the other male members of the group into line behind them.

"Come along, Madoc. Tail on to the rope with the rest of us. Herbert, Cyril, Donald, take your places. Lawrence, are you ready? Where's that young chap who came with Val?"

"Where's Val, for that matter?" drawled May. "Lost her eyelashes?"

"She was putting them on when I left her just now," Janet answered. "I expect she'll be right along."

"Then you don't know Vallie like I do. Call her, Babs, before Squire has apoplexy."

"Hark!"

A hand grabbed Janet's arm and she jumped. "They're coming now. Can't you hear them?"

Janet couldn't see how anybody could distinguish one sound from another in this babble, unless it was a bray like May's. Moreover, she didn't like having her arm clutched and her ear hissed into. She was about to pull away when she realized the grabber was an elderly woman who, for a wonder, was not wearing a wool skirt and pullover but an old-fashioned dinner gown of rubbed wine-colored velvet.

Perhaps this was Mrs. Squire. Then again, perhaps it wasn't. The hand on her arm bore several antique garnet and opal rings, but no plain gold band.

"How do you do?" she said. "I don't believe we've met. I'm Janet Wadman."

"Ah, but you won't be for long. You're going to be married much sooner than you think, and it won't be the way you planned it, either. It's all happened faster than you expected, but never you mind. You're the only one in the world for him and he's the one for you and there's nobody going to talk you out of it, though there's somebody who's going to try. Look, I told you he was coming. What did you ever see in a thing like that?"

"I've often wondered."

Janet was not really surprised to see who'd got himself invited to Graylings as Valerie Condrycke's escort. After all, Val was a board member's daughter and Roy Robbins couldn't rise far on looks and charm unless he applied them in higher places than the typing pool.

Roy himself went into shock when he caught sight of Janet. His eyes looked glazed as he turned his head away and let himself be hustled across the floor by Squire. It hadn't been good office politics getting off on the wrong foot with the head of the family first crack off the bat like this. Perhaps she ought to give him a hint for auld lang syne.

It seemed unbelievable to Janet, watching Roy tag on to the rope behind Madoc, that a year ago this time she'd fancied herself in love with that shop-window dummy. She'd been flattered, she supposed, and too green to know better. At least she'd had sense enough to learn from the experience. She wondered whether Val would. No sense in trying to tell her, of course. But how had this odd old woman known about herself and Roy, and about her hurried-up engagement? Who was she, anyway?

There was no time now to ask. The men on the rope were pulling a great log across the floor. It lay on a well-waxed skid and must not be all that difficult to move, though everybody except Madoc was putting on a great show of slaving at the task. Rhys was only looking gently amused and quite remarkably handsome, Janet thought, among this lot of blond beeves. Roy was going to be just like the Condryckes in a few years; still a fine-looking chap, no doubt, but too thick around the beltline and running to jowl at the jaws. He'd got over his astonishment now and was grunting and groaning with the best of them while the women cheered them on.

Suddenly Janet wasn't tired any more. She was laughing and clapping while Squire and his crew with great fanfare rolled the Yule log into the fireplace and set it alight. She was running across the Great Hall to hug her sweetheart, knowing she was his and the odd old lady was right forever and ever, amen. On the whole, she was rather pleased than not that Roy was here, because now she knew she'd never have to give him another thought, but only a pleasant nod and smile as she would any casual acquaintance.

"Hello, Roy. Happy Yuletide. Is that the proper thing to say, Squire?"

"Oh, do you two know each other?"

"Of course. I used to type up his letters."

"And correct my spelling." Roy was himself now, all teeth and personality.

"But now she brings me my tea." Donald laid a hand on each of their shoulders. "Though not for long, I'm afraid. Janet's about to retire from the business world. Right, Madoc?"

"Couldn't be righter. She'll be giving you her notice for a Christmas box. Mother's ordered us to start house hunting forthwith."

"And when Lady Rhys commands, you obey, eh?"

"Not always, I'm afraid. But this is one time when we're quite willing to be dutiful children. Eh, Jenny love?" Madoc slipped an arm around Janet and gently detached her from Donald's grasp.

"Shall you be living here or going back to Britain?" Squire asked.

"We shall be staying in Fredericton, at least for the time

being. My parents keep a place in Winnipeg that we'll probably use sometimes and I expect we'll go over to visit my great-uncle as soon as the Canadian government feels it can manage without me for a week or two. Our plans are a bit up in the air at the moment. So are we. Ah, what is this?"

"Here I come awassailing," caroled May, holding aloft a steaming silver bowl the size of a washbasin. She must be strong as a bull moose. "Squire, come and do the honors. We're all dying of thirst."

She set the bowl down on an ebony and ormolu table that already held a vast silver tray, an ornate ladle, and an array of crystal cups. Squire plunged the ladle into the bowl and brought it up full. The old lady in velvet shrieked and fainted. Everybody else broke into whoops of merriment.

"Well, Cyril complained last year that a wassail bowl's supposed to have roasted crabs in it," May said with a feigned air of injured innocence. "I couldn't find any crabs at the market so I used plastic spiders instead. They look much the same now that I've roasted them."

"I meant crab apples, you jackass," replied her brother affectionately. "Come on, let's not waste good liquor. Chuck 'em out and start baling. We've got to toast the newlyweds."

"They're not wed yet," Clara contradicted him.

"Good. That means we get to toast them again next time. Do you suppose somebody ought to cut Aunt Adelaide's corset strings?"

"I'll tuck a pillow under her head," said Babs kindly. "She'll come round in a minute. Val dear, do be careful where you step in those high heels. You know how Aunt Addie hates being trodden on while she's in a swoon."

"But shouldn't we at least try smelling salts or spirits of ammonia?" Janet was appalled at this cavalier attitude.

"Oh, we wouldn't think of it," Val assured her. "Aunt Addie enjoys fainting, she does it so beautifully. It would be a shame to spoil her fun too soon, so we always let her lie.

Have to humor the old folks, you know. By the way, where's Granny?"

"Good Lord yes, where is she?" cried Squire. "This is terrible. Granny's never missed the bringing in of the Yule log before. Run up and see if she's in her room. No, wait, you mustn't miss the toasts. Ludovic! Ludovic, where—oh, there you are. Go find out why Mrs. Condrycke isn't down here with the rest of us."

CHAPTER 4

Squire went on ladling wassail and passing around the crystal cups while the old retainer, for Ludovic was surely that, zigzagged up the incredible staircase out in the front hall. No wonder this family was so prone to jokes, Janet thought. Graylings was a joke in itself.

Ludovic was no joke, though. He could have passed for a Presbyterian minister in his sober black suit, black tie, and dazzling white linen. He was tallish, though by no means so big as the Condryckes; thinner and grayer and craggier in the features and infinitely graver of countenance. His shoulders were stooped as if from a lifetime of carrying trays, and he had a habit of looking a hair's breadth to the left of whomever he happened to be facing, as though it wasn't the done thing for a servant to look those he served full in the eyes.

Janet supposed Ludovic must be the butler. She'd never seen one in the flesh before. The closest they came to one at the farm was Sam Neddick, who sat down to meals with the rest of them and expected to be waited on by the womenfolk just like Bert. She smiled to herself. Madoc, who had been feasting his eyes on his beloved since nobody had yet given him anything to feed his face with, asked her what was so funny.

"I was just wondering what Ludovic would say if I told him to haul up a chair while I cut him a piece of pie."

"Jenny love, have I happened to mention lately that I adore you?"

"It's always nice to be reminded."

"Er—that chap Roy. Is he . . . ?"

"Madoc, you surely don't think you've caught me on the rebound? Yes, he's the one, but don't bother poking him in the jaw on my account. Feel free to do it on your own if you care to, of course. I'll bet you once fell for a girl like Val."

"How did you know?"

"Because you looked at her the same way I've been feeling about Roy. Relieved and puzzled."

This time they laughed together. May demanded to know why.

"Come on, you two, no private jokes. What's so funny?"

"Nothing much," Janet told her composedly. "We're simply enjoying ourselves. What's in this punch? It smells divine."

"Heavens, child, don't call it punch or the water kelpies will get you. That's the wassail and I wish Granny would get a move on because my tongue's hanging out. We don't dare take a swallow till Squire fires the starting pistol. Everybody got some? Watch it, Cyril. Only one to a customer."

"Then why don't we just hand him the bowl?" quipped Herbert. "Ah, here's Ludovic. Where is she, Lewd?"

"Mrs. Condrycke regrets that she is unable to join the party," the butler reported.

"Why? She's not sick is she?" asked Babs.

"No, madam. Mrs. Condrycke has misplaced her dentures and does not care to appear without them."

"Oh, poor Granny!"

But Babs couldn't help laughing and neither could anybody else. At last Squire wiped his eyes on a monogrammed linen handkerchief and said, "Then take one up to her, Ludovic, and we'll toast her *in absentia*. Ready, everyone? To Granny, and a speedy recovery."

"Not too speedy," said Lawrence. "At least for the moment we can be reasonably sure her bark is worse than her bite."

But he didn't say it loudly and hardly anyone heard him except Madoc Rhys, who began to wonder about Granny.

There were any number of other toasts. Either each was funnier than the one before or else the wassail was pretty strong. Janet suspected the latter and drank her toasts in the tiniest possible sips. Madoc nursed his along, too, but nobody else was showing much restraint. Even Aunt Adelaide had risen from her swoon in time to join in the wassail and was swigging away with the best of them. All of a sudden, she grabbed Clara by the arm and cried, "Hark!"

"Is it out there?" cried Cyril in delight.

"It's coming! I can feel it."

"Draw the curtains, quick."

Everybody rushed to pull aside the heavy draperies that had been drawn close to keep out the drafts from the large front windows.

"What's happening?" Janet asked Clara. "I don't see anything."

"Wait. It's coming. Aunt Addie always knows."

"Look!" shouted Val. "There it is."

Janet caught her breath. Not having grown up along the coast, she'd never seen a fire ship, although tales of these sea-going specters were rife in New Brunswick waters. But she'd heard tales enough, and she knew at once what she was seeing now. The Phantom Ship of Bay Chaleur was no fairy tale. How silently it came; how swiftly; how terrifying its eerie glow. She could see flames licking at the shrouds, yet each mast and spar stood out clearly against the snow-covered rocks that ringed the bay for an instant before it vanished.

"I can't believe it," she murmured.

"You're in luck, Janet," Squire told her jovially. "Some people live out their whole lives around the Bay Chaleur and never once set eyes on the Phantom Ship. Some say it's the ghost of a vessel called the *John Craig,* which was wrecked in a gale sometime during the eighteenth century. Some claim it's a French ship, burned to keep it from falling into British hands during the Battle of the Restigouche. About seventeen-sixty, that would be. Anyway, I'm glad we were able to give you the treat."

"Do you see it often, Squire?"

May answered Janet's question for her father. "No, thank God. The ship is no treat to me, I can tell you. The first time I ever saw it, I fell off my horse the very next morning and broke my leg. The second was the night of the big gale that wrecked my boat and knocked down a big hackmatack that came right through my bedroom window and scared me half to death."

"And the third time you married Herbert," said Clara not quite so playfully as she might have. "Remember? I came down with measles and crashed the reception with spots all over me and gave them to Herbert and put a crimp in your honeymoon."

"Clara always had an original sense of humor," Squire laughed indulgently. "Come along, everybody, drink up. Ludovic, isn't it almost time we went into the dining room?"

"Yes, sir. I was about to announce dinner when the fire ship arrived."

"Well, let's hope if the ship portends another disaster, it isn't to the dinner," said Lawrence. "I'm starved."

"When are you not?" His playful wife gave the lawyer a poke in the paunch. "All hands round and do-si-do. Last one in's a rotten egg."

In fact, they formed up decorously enough. Squire gave his arm to Janet, which was an honor she hadn't anticipated and could have done nicely without, although her status as a bride-to-be entitled her to it, she supposed. Madoc offered his to Aunt Adelaide as the eldest of the ladies, somewhat to the chagrin of Valerie, who had been eyeing Dafydd's younger brother with a certain amount of interest despite Roy's toothsome presence. The rest paired off one way and another, all but Cyril. He made a last detour past the wassail bowl before winding up the procession with May's sons Edwin and Francis, whom their elders thought it fun to call Winny and Franny though Ed and Frank would no doubt have pleased the boys better.

Babs had not exaggerated about the tons of lovely food.

Janet would have been willing to call it quits after the oyster soup, but there was still the roast goose and a good deal more to come. The Condryckes ate as lustily as they drank. Janet and Madoc couldn't possibly begin to keep up, though they both had healthy enough appetites for smallish people. They made jokes about not being able to get into their wedding clothes if they overstuffed and managed to avoid surfeit without giving offense, or so they hoped.

"What a pity about your grandmother's teeth," Janet remarked to Donald, who was sitting on her other side. "You must be sorry she had to miss dinner."

"Oh, Granny never eats with the family," he replied. "She has a sort of high tea at five o'clock or thereabout, and a snack at bedtime if she feels like it. She's quite old, you know. Though come to think of it, how could you know? Perhaps Babs or May will take you and Madoc up to meet her after we finish, if she's not asleep and has managed to find her teeth. Granny's much too vain to show herself without them. She was a beauty in her day, and she still likes to be thought one. Are you quite sure you don't want Ludovic to give you another sliver of goose?"

"Really, I couldn't," she assured him. "I'm sure there's a wonderful dessert to come and I'm trying to save room for a taste."

"There is and you must. Babs is right, I always do have to diet after a visit to Graylings. She keeps me on bread and water at home. Don't you, Babs?" Donald called across the table to his wife.

"As her lawyer I advise her not to answer that," shouted Lawrence, who was sitting next to his sister-in-law. He was pretty well flown by now. Ludovic had been keeping the glasses filled with what was probably very good wine, although all Janet knew about wine was that it made her sleepy if she drank much and she was already having trouble keeping her eyes open. She motioned Ludovic away when he brought the bottle back to her.

Madoc was doing the same, she noticed. That was just as well. Dessert turned out to be a trifle so lavishly soaked in rum that the mere smell was enough to turn one's head. It was a pity Squire didn't carry his penchant for the good old ways far enough to keep a few wolfhounds under the table so there'd be a place to dispose of some excess food.

Donald ate his trifle with no fuss about calories. He seemed pleased with himself tonight, and Janet couldn't help wondering if his self-satisfaction had anything to do with his having been able to snare a distinguished guest for Squire. It was hard for her to think of Madoc as a celebrity, but she supposed he was, after a fashion.

Squire at any rate was making the most of Madoc's connections. "What a pity Lady Rhys had to dash off to London instead of coming up to join the party. David tells me she's quite a personage in her own right."

"Oh, she is," Janet replied, feeling a bit fuzzy on account of the trifle. "Did you know she once sang a concert for the Queen Mother?"

"No! You must tell me all about it."

"Madoc can do that better than I."

"Then let's move to where we can be cozy. May, if everyone's finished, don't you think it's time we had our coffee?"

"If they're not finished, they darn well ought to be." May swung her parrot around to reveal a watch set into its rump. "It's half past ten, egad. Or do I mean forsooth? Get your nose out of the trough, Lawrence. There doesn't seem to be anything left to eat anyway. I move we take the coffee into the library, Squire. The Great Hall must be colder than Greenland's icy mountains by now. All those in favor say aye. The rest keep quiet because nobody's listening."

That was true enough and had been for most of the evening. By and large, the Condryckes seemed more concerned to outshout each other than to engage in any real communication. May at her loudest couldn't manage to collect everyone's attention until Babs caught Janet's eye and rose.

Janet most gratefully followed her example, then Clara, Aunt Adelaide, and Val. Madoc shoved back his chair and managed to get next to Janet as they at last left the banqueting board.

"I thought the gentlemen were supposed to stay and guzzle port after the ladies left," she teased.

"I've guzzled enough for one night, thanks. How are you bearing up?"

"I'll be all right so long as I don't have to swallow one more mouthful of anything for the next week or so. Where on earth do you suppose they put it all?"

He glanced at Lawrence's magisterial paunch. "Isn't that rather obvious?"

She giggled and Roy, who was now well over the line, turned around to give Madoc a remarkably dirty look. Did he think they were laughing about him? No matter. Madoc had sense enough not to tackle a drunk on the strength of a sneer, especially when they were both guests in somebody else's house. And likely to be stormed in by morning if the ghost ship was reliable in its predictions. The wind had picked up while they were at dinner, and the air had smelled like snow when they'd got out of the helicopter.

Not that snow could be any novelty in these parts and not that it made any difference anyway. Squire obviously kept Graylings well stocked with provender, the woods were full of fuel, and the house must be remarkably well-built to have withstood so many winters already.

This house party wasn't turning out as anticipated, but nobody could call it dull. Madoc and his Jenny found a nice, squashy chesterfield far enough from the tall stove to keep from getting boiled alive and settled themselves in one corner.

"All set for a quiet cuddle, eh?" boomed May.

Madoc nudged himself even closer to Janet. "Sit with us and chaperon," he invited.

"Can't. I have to pour the coffee. Here, Aunt Addie, come and keep an eye on these two."

That was a desirable arrangement, as Aunt Addie at once fell asleep in the opposite corner of the sofa. By now everybody was showing the somnolescent effects of all that food and drink. The general hilarity had subsided, more or less. Herbert was telling a long story that didn't seem to have much point. Lawrence was grunting and trying to loosen his trouser button without being too obvious about it. What the rest were doing, Madoc neither knew nor cared. He was watching his Jenny sip from a tiny Royal Doulton cup and thinking what a dainty dish she'd make to set before the Queen. Jenny would be dozing herself any second now, preferably in the crook of his arm with her head on his shoulder.

"Warm enough, love?" he murmured into her hair.

"M'm. I like this room."

"What was that, Janet?" Squire called out. "I'm sorry, I didn't hear."

Why should he have heard? She wasn't speaking to him. Perhaps she ought to have been.

"I was just saying how much I like your library."

"I expect you'll be living in a much grander house than this one day. Eh, Madoc?"

"Do you mean the family place in Wales? Not a chance, I'm afraid, unless I bump off two uncles and three cousins of whom I'm rather fond, not to mention my own father and elder brother. Younger sons of younger sons don't come in for ancestral acres. Janet's not expecting any elaborate layout. Are you, Jenny love?"

"Certainly I am. My brother's already promised us a bearskin rug just like yours, Squire." Janet buried the toes of her evening slippers in the warm fur at her feet. "I hope it's a friendly one. This is the happiest bear I've ever—good heavens, no wonder! Would those by any chance happen to be your grandmother's teeth it's wearing?"

CHAPTER 5

That livened up the party. Even Aunt Adelaide woke and managed a few polite snickers before dropping off again.

"Poor Granny," gasped Babs, wiping her eyes. "Whoever would do a thing like this to her?"

"Those two whelps of mine, I shouldn't be surprised." Herbert sounded very much the proud father. "I'll haul 'em over the coals for this."

"Not too hard, Bert," said his father-in-law benignly. "It's Christmas, after all. Or will be, the day after tomorrow."

"And you can't say they haven't made us merry," Clara added. "Where did they skip off to after dinner, anyway? I've barely had a chance to say hello to them since they got home from school."

"Why should you complain? Neither have I and I'm their mother," May replied. "I suppose they're off to the billiard room again. I might as well have given birth to a couple of cue balls. Eighteen months lugging those kids around and what have I to show for it? Stretch marks on my tum and chalk on my thumb. More coffee, anyone? Brandy? Crème de menthe? Crème de cacao? Crème de la crème?"

"Rhys will have some of that," said Roy, smiling ever so bewitchingly to show he was joking. "Sorry, Janet. I'm afraid you don't think that was amusing."

"Don't I?" If Roy thought he was going to get a rise out of her, he'd better think again. "Say it again and I'll try to stay awake long enough to listen. Do forgive me, everyone. I don't know if it's that gorgeous dinner or the wassail or the traveling or the fact that I got about three hours' sleep last night, but I seem to be a little bit drowsy. Did you want Madoc and me to go up and meet your grandmother, Donald, now that she's got her teeth back?"

"Are we sure the bear can bear to part with them?" Cyril wanted to know.

"Yes, let's get the bear facts," Lawrence added owlishly.

"You're both unbearable," Babs told them. "What do you think, May? It's rather late, isn't it? Will she be awake?"

"Who knows?"

May was pouring herself a tot of crème de menthe, green to match her parrot, and didn't sound as if she cared, either.

"If you want my advice for what it's worth," said Clara, "you'll slip those teeth back on her nightstand and make believe they were there all the time and she simply overlooked seeing them. Otherwise we'll have the father and mother of a row. You know Granny."

"Don't we ever!" sighed Val. "I vote with Aunt Clara. Am I old enough to have a vote, Squire?"

"I vote with you in any case, Vallie," he assured her. "We certainly don't want Granny too upset to enjoy the mumming tomorrow night. You know how she loves to dress up. And now, Janet my dear, you will not outrage my sense of hospitality if you betake yourself upstairs. Nor you, Madoc, since I expect you'd find things dull down here without her."

"Not at all," the younger son of the younger son replied courteously, "but I may as well make sure she doesn't get lost on that remarkable staircase of yours. It's been a thoroughly delightful evening, Squire, and I look forward to tomorrow as I'm sure Janet does, too. Good night, everyone."

"I'll come with you," said Babs, "and I strongly recommend that you come too, Donald. You might give an arm to Aunt Addie while you're about it. We do exhaust her, poor dear. Vallie, why don't you take Roy down to the billiard room with Franny and Winny if you're going to stay up for a while? Clara, are you coming? Good night, Squire darling. It's been marvelous as always."

"Wait a second," cried May. "Who gets to bell the cat?"

"You mean put Granny's teeth back? I will if you like."

"Then who's to put Aunt Addie to bed?" Donald protested. "I don't mind helping her into her nightie, you understand, but she might resent my attentions."

"I'll do Aunt Addie, then, and Clara can manage the teeth," said his wife. "Anyone else care to join the expedition?"

"Lawrence will," said Clara. "If he goes to sleep in that chair he'll wake about two o'clock with a case of lumbago and claim it's all my fault. Up, sluggard!"

Lawrence upped, somewhat unsteadily. Clara took her husband's arm with an efficiency born, Janet suspected, of much practice, and steered him up those incredible stairs to the room that was evidently set aside for them.

"Get to bed, Lawrence," she ordered. "I'll be along in a minute," and came out of the room with the teeth in her hand.

They next deposited Aunt Addie, by now more or less awake and protesting that she could manage perfectly well by herself, thank you.

"Then we'll leave you here," said Donald, opening another door for Babs.

"Oh, no you won't," Clara protested. "What if she wakes up and attacks me with her cane?"

"I'll come." Babs was beginning to sound frazzled around the edges. "Donald, you needn't."

"Would she actually hit you?" asked Madoc, much interested.

"She would and then some," Clara assured him. "You don't know Granny."

"I'm looking forward to meeting her."

"I can't imagine why, but come along if you like. Your rooms are down near hers anyway."

"Have you got your bearings yet?" Babs added. "See, this end of the hall fans out into a sort of hexagonal bay.

The bathrooms are clustered around the inside walls and your rooms are on the outside. Franny and Winny have the two beyond Val's and Granny has the two at the far end. The children are here so little, you see, except during their holidays from boarding school, that it's quiet most of the time. Granny sleeps in the big room that corresponds to Val's, and uses the little one beside it for a sitting room."

"It's a convenient arrangement," said Clara, "for everybody. Why's she got her door shut, I wonder?"

"She didn't want anyone to barge in and catch her without her teeth, of course. Go ahead, Clara. We'll stay out here, just in case. I'm sure she's asleep by now, though."

Janet hoped so. She was ready to drop on her feet, and feeling a trifle annoyed with Madoc for being so darned polite. Surely Granny would rather meet them fresh and rested tomorrow morning.

"I wonder if I should take the lamp?" Clara sounded so nervous one might have thought she was confronting a caged lion. "I shouldn't think so, unless Herbert's been doing tricks with hers. Lawrence and I got one of those battery-operated table lamps for Granny," she explained to Janet and Madoc, "because we've been so afraid she might upset an oil lamp. She doesn't see too well, and you know how dangerous those things can be if they fall and break, especially in an old wooden house like Graylings."

"Clara, quit stalling," said Babs, rather amused. "You can give your fire prevention lecture some other time."

"All right. Wish me luck."

Clara smoothed down her beige and blue skirt and edged the door open. "Granny," she called softly, "are you awake? Gran—Babs, come here!"

"Here, hold this." Babs quickly handed the oil lamp she was carrying to Madoc and ran into the bedroom. "Clara, what's the matter? Is she—oh, Clara!"

Madoc stepped quietly into the room. Janet, not caring to be left alone in the dark, followed him.

"Excuse me," he murmured. "I've had a little first-aid training. Can I help?"

"Nothing's going to help her now." Clara's voice was shaking. "She's ice cold."

The old woman hanging half out of the high tester bed might have been a beauty once. Now she was frightful to look at. Her eyes were staring, her toothless mouth agape, her sparse white hair hanging down over her face in wispy locks.

"Where's her nightcap?" Clara asked stupidly.

"Here on the floor. It must have fallen off when she . . ." Babs bent to pick up the frilly white cap, and stood turning it over in her hands.

"I'd made her a new one for Christmas," she said dully. "Well, I suppose at her age it was bound to happen. We ought to be relieved she went so quickly. She must have been all right when Ludovic took the wassail up to her, otherwise he'd surely have said something. Look, here's the little tray with the silver pitcher and the cup she drank out of, right here on the nightstand."

"There's still some left in the pitcher," said Clara. "That's not like Granny."

"Maybe she decided to save that last bit for a nightcap."

"Oh, yes, that would be it. And she was reaching out to get it when she . . ." Clara shook her head as if to clear it. "Do you think we ought to tell the others?"

"I don't know." Babs hesitated. "It's so late. Squire must have gone to his room by now. I hate to spoil his night's rest. It isn't as if anybody could do anything, and you know what it would be like if we got them all milling around again."

"But his own mother . . ."

Janet caught herself. This was family business. She had no right to pass an opinion.

"Granny was only Squire's mother-in-law." That seemed to clinch it for Clara. "Madoc, I hate to ask, but would you mind lifting her back on the bed? I don't think I could . . ."

"Of course." He set down the lamp next to the wassail tray, then gently laid the old woman's body back among the eyelet-embroidered down pillows and drew the lace-edged sheet up over her face.

"I'll shut the damper on the stove." Babs was herself again, calmly efficient. "The colder we keep the room—oh, God! Of all the times for this to happen. It's awful, I know, but that's all I can think of. Squire loves his Christmas so, and May breaks her back to have everything the way he wants it. And you do so much, Clara," she added before her sister-in-law could point out this fact herself. "We simply mustn't let this put a damper on the whole holiday. Granny wouldn't have wanted that, would she?"

"God knows what Granny would have wanted. I just hope May doesn't take a notion to look in here. You know the kind of hullabaloo she'd raise. Come on, Babs, let's shut the door and turn the key. I'm half dead myself and you must be, too. Maybe in the morning we'll be able to think straight."

They turned off the battery lamp and went out into the chilly hallway again. Janet was relieved that her room was nearest. Val must still be downstairs with Roy, but somebody had been in while the family were at dinner to pull out the trundle bed and turn back its warm flannelette sheets.

She gave Madoc a goodnight kiss at the door and changed quickly into her night things. The room was so cold she put on her thermal underwear under a long-sleeved granny gown. She left her pearls on, too, tucked in against her skin to keep them warm. Then she made a hurried trip to the bathroom and rushed back to the trundle bed. Let Val have the one she was used to. By now, Janet would have been content to stretch out on a picket fence.

Madoc went to bed, too, but he was less exhausted than Janet. He had in his career developed the useful faculty of grabbing a few minutes' sleep here and there as occasion permitted. He'd slept a good bit on the helicopter coming up and sneaked several catnaps under cover of the general hilarity during that long dinner and the gathering in the library afterward.

An hour or so later, when he judged the household was settled down for the night, he woke himself up, slid out of bed, and put on heavy sheepskin-lined slippers and a most wonderful bathrobe warmly handwoven of wool grown on that vast family estate in Wales he would never, God willing, fall heir to. As he was brushing his hair and tying the sash, for he was a tidy man by nature, Rhys heard a small commotion in the next room. Val was still up, blast her, and from the sound of things she was waking his Jenny. He couldn't make out what they were saying for the door was heavily built and weather-stripped against drafts, but it became clear when Janet, in blue knitted bedsocks and a fleecy blue robe, opened the door and came into his room.

"Val's expecting company," she muttered. "I'm sorry, Madoc. I didn't know what else to do. She seems to think we'd . . ."

He put his arms around her. "And you don't, do you?"

"Not like this."

She had her head on his chest and the situation would have been most agreeable under different circumstances. "Madoc, you know I wouldn't have said I'd marry you if I didn't want to be a wife to you. I want it so much I . . ." she shivered and pressed herself closer. "But not in some stranger's house while my old boyfriend's having fun and games with the girl next door. That's not how I want to remember the most precious night of my life. But where shall I go?"

"You shall hop into that bed, which I've got nicely warmed for you, and I shall take my gentlemanly departure, which I was about to do in any case. Don't fret yourself about what may be happening in the next room. Your old boyfriend's tight as a drum. If I may say so without offending your sense of propriety, I think Miss Val is due for a sad disappointment."

"Serves her right. Where are you going?"

"For a walk. Now hush yourself and go to sleep. I'll probably wind up on that comfortable chesterfield in the library."

"But you'll freeze to death."

"Not I, Jenny love. I shall put more wood in the stove, open the damper, and wrap myself in a nice, thick afghan I saw down there. If I'm still cold, I'll add the bearskin rug. I've slept in worse places."

He tucked her up, still wearing her fleecy robe, kissed her goodnight in a chaste and fatherly manner, and eased himself out of the room. There was a small flashlight in his bathrobe pocket but he didn't use it. Sure enough, a moment later a large young man stepped out of one of the bathrooms and made his somewhat unsteady way across the hall. Rhys waited until he'd made damn sure Roy had got into the room where Val was expecting him, then slid along the dark walls toward the two-room suite that was now occupied by one stiffening corpse.

CHAPTER 6

Nobody else was visiting Granny. The lamp Babs had extinguished in a probably unconscious gesture of finality when they'd left the dead woman to herself was still off. Rhys would have liked to turn it on again but there was no telling who might be having to use the nearby bathroom and whether the gleam would be noticed under the door. He made do with the little pocket flash that he could shield with his robe as he examined the body.

Rhys was no doctor. Still, he'd seen a good many corpses in his relatively short but somewhat crowded career. He'd also seen odd coincidences that turned out to be nothing of the sort. The combination of the missing teeth and the abrupt demise of their owner in the space of a few hours was not the sort of thing someone of his profession could dismiss without question. It was a terrible breach of hospitality, no doubt, to be wondering which member of his host family had bumped off Granny, but he'd eat his badge if she'd died without help.

The old lady didn't appear to have been diabetic, especially since she'd been quaffing Squire's wassail. There were no needle marks or any other marks except those normally associated with age and decay. There was no wound of any kind, no odor of bitter almonds hovering about the lips. There were other odors not usually mentioned in detective stories but familiar to law enforcement officers who have to deal with the suddenly dead. They'd have to burn the mattress, probably.

He might collect a specimen of fecal matter for analysis, but he doubted whether that would reveal anything. According to Donald, Granny had eaten her last meal about half past five. Judging from the evidence she'd had nothing since then but the wassail. If she'd rung for a snack later on, whoever brought it would no doubt have poured that last drain of wassail into the cup for her to drink before she went to sleep, if that was what she'd had in mind, and taken away the empty pitcher. He could take a sample of the wassail, too, but the odds were it wouldn't show anything, either. Otherwise it wouldn't have been left.

Granny had been a big woman in her day, but age had shrunk her to some extent. She must have been not less than eighty and more likely a good way beyond. Maybe those yarns the Condryckes told about Granny's being wont to lay about her with her cane were true, but the chances that she'd had strength enough in those wizened arms to do any real damage were slim.

Here lay no sturdy peasant woman who'd been used to hard work all her life, but a pampered lady used to luxury and ease, as her surroundings attested. If that was her picture on the dresser, she must indeed have been a beauty, and therefore, being of the generation who went in for lily-white complexions and slender, tapered hands, no active sportswoman. She'd probably never developed any real muscle; certainly there was no sign of it now. She wouldn't have been much good at defending herself in a struggle. In the unlikely event that he himself had felt any urge to kill a weak old woman like her, he'd simply have covered her face with one of these soft down pillows she had about her in such abundance and held it there until she stopped breathing.

Or perhaps not a pillow. Suppose, for instance, Granny had slopped some of the wassail over her chin. She very well might have if that pitcher had been anywhere near full when Ludovic took it up to her. The receptacle was no dainty toy. It must hold a good three cupfuls. There wasn't more than half an inch or so left in the bottom now, and that potation had been potent beyond belief. Say she'd been lying there sloshed to the eyeballs with a sticky mess on her chin. One of her playful descendants, or the spouse of one, had come up to use the bathroom as they'd all done at one time or another during the evening. What could be more natural than for that person to drop in on poor Granny, exiled from the festivities by the absence of her false teeth, and offer to tidy her up?

She'd have accepted the attention willingly enough, no doubt, or at least not have been able to resist it. A wet face towel folded into a smallish pad would make a most useful tool to smother somebody with. Being damp, it would cling more tightly to the nose and mouth and be less apt to shed fluff into her lungs when she struggled for breath. After the deed was done, it need only be rinsed in case it bore any tell-tale traces of saliva or vomit and then dropped down the laundry chute with scads of other wet towels.

Rhys felt the face and hair. Sure enough, the skin was clean but some of the straggling wisps around the mouth felt stiff and ropy, as if they might well have been dampened by the spiced, sweetened wassail and not washed off afterward. He found a pair of nail scissors and a tissue on the dressing table, cut off a snippet where it wasn't apt to be noticed, and wrapped it in the tissue for safekeeping.

Then he checked the pillows. Yes, there was a stain on one of the pillowcases and yes, it smelled like the stuff in the pitcher. That didn't mean Granny had been killed lying on this pillow, but neither did it mean she hadn't. She couldn't have died in the position where she'd been found. That would have been a most unhandy way to smother anybody to begin with, and would have meant she'd struggled against her killer. Rhys didn't think Granny had put up any sort of fight. There were no bruises, no signs of blood or flesh under the finger-nails she'd kept buffed to a high shine and filed to neat crescents. None of them was broken, and old nails were brittle. It was dollars to doughnuts she'd been smothered lying flat on her back, then flopped over to look as though she'd been reaching for that last swig of wassail when she'd taken a seizure of some kind and died. Maybe this was some Condrycke's notion of the ultimate practical joke.

Rhys felt a strong disinclination to stay in this room any longer. He snapped off his handy little torch and backed silently out the door, locking it again after him with the key he'd brought from his own room on the perfectly correct assumption that all these old bedroom locks worked the same.

Caution was well advised. He'd rounded two bends of the hexagon when Valerie's bedroom door opened and Roy came out, looking not at all the conquering hero. From his vantage point in the shadows, Rhys could see Val sitting up in the tumbled bed, wearing only a petulant expression. He found the spectacle unimpressive.

Not bothering to get up and close the door, Val reached for a robe that was hanging over the footboard and put it on. Then she cocked a speculative eye at the connecting door behind which Janet was presumably rapt in well-deserved slumber. She slid her feet to the floor, groped for a pair of slippers, then padded over to close the door into the hall. Rhys then moved toward the door that should have been his own and edged it open a crack, just in time to hear Val's cry.

"Surprise!"

She had a flashlight in one hand and a fistful of blankets in the other. There on the stripped bed lay Janet in her blue fleece cocoon, complete with flannel nightgown, thermal underwear, bedsocks, pearls, and diamond engagement ring, rubbing her knuckles into her eyes like a waking baby.

"Where's Madoc?" said Val stupidly.

"On the couch in the library catching pneumonia." Janet sounded much put out, as she had reason to.

"Why? Did you have a fight or something?"

"Of course not!"

"Then what is this, one of those marriage of convenience things? He's homosexual, right?"

"Wrong. We simply didn't want to abuse your family's hospitality by doing something we shouldn't have cared to get caught at, which turned out to be a good thing for us, didn't it? And I can't say I care for being waked up at odd hours and shoved from pillar to post, so would you kindly make up your mind where I'm to sleep and let me get on with it?"

"Some party this is turning out to be! You'd better come back in with me, I suppose. Ludovic comes around with tea at the crack of dawn and Squire will have fits if we're not where we're supposed to be."

"Then give me that flashlight and go on back to bed. I'll try to find Madoc."

"What if you meet Squire?"

"I'll tell him I'm walking in my sleep."

Janet took the blankets from Val and put Madoc's bed to rights with a few deft flaps and tucks, then reached out her hand for the torch. "Go ahead. I'll light you through."

Val looked Janet up and down as she surrendered the light. "You know, you look as if you wouldn't say boo to a mouse."

"I don't suppose I would. What would be the sense? Do get a move on."

Madoc waited in the dark until Valerie Condrycke had shut the door between the two bedrooms, then stepped inside with his finger across his lips. Janet, bless her staunch little heart, goggled for an instant, then ran over to him.

"I might have known you were here all the time," she breathed into his neck.

"Actually I wasn't. I just happened to be passing by as the party was breaking up next door. Give Val a few minutes to get nicely asleep, then you can go wake her up and tell her you found me."

The few minutes passed pleasantly. It was with considerable reluctance that Madoc said at last, "Jenny love, you'd better go now or I shall be overcoming my scruples. You don't really intend to make me wait for the relatives to lay on a fancy wedding?"

"I couldn't turn you down twice in one night, could I? Anyway, Aunt Adelaide told me this evening we'd marry earlier than we planned. It wouldn't be polite to make a liar out of her, would it?"

"Rudest thing in the world."

Rhys tested his scruples a moment longer, then pushed Janet gently toward the door. "Sleep well, my darling."

"Where will you be?"

"Right here, dreaming about you."

"Good." Janet kissed him once more and went.

Val must be either sleeping or sulking. Rhys listened for possible sounds of altercation, but there were none. Janet had got back into the trundle bed and, he hoped, to peaceful slumber without a sound. He himself lay thinking the thoughts of a young man in love about whether his Jenny would wear her blue knitted bedsocks on their wedding night, and the thoughts of a detective inspector about who had killed Squire Condrycke's mother-in-law, and why. At length he reminded himself there was nothing more he could do about either murder or matrimony at this hour of the morning and went to sleep himself.

CHAPTER 7

It was dull gray when Rhys woke up. However, the wristwatch he was still wearing said nine o'clock and Ludovic was standing over him with the cup of hot tea as advertised. On impulse, he addressed the man in Welsh.

"Thank you and a good morning. Or is it?"

Ludovic actually smiled, and replied in the same language. "Ah, sir, it is long since I have heard that tongue spoken. And never before in this house. A good morning to you, sir, although in fact it is not. The fire ship was again a portent of storm."

"Storm within or storm without?"

"It is strange that you ask. Are you one of those who know?"

"No, I am one of those who are supposed to find out. What is happening?"

"It is snowing heavily and there has been a death in the family. The old lady whom you heard referred to as Granny and was in fact the relict of the present Condrycke family's late grandfather has passed away peacefully in her sleep."

"That, as a matter of fact, I did know. My fiancée and I happened to be with Mrs. Clara and Mrs. Donald when they found her dead in bed last night."

Rhys sipped at his tea, its steam noticeable in the cold room. "They had gone in to return the teeth Miss Wadman found, as you have perhaps been told. Mrs. Clara decided not to tell the rest until morning, so we of course respected her wish. Has Squire now been told?"

"Oh yes, sir. Squire would normally have been informed at once of any untoward occurrence. He is somewhat cast down by the prospect that the late Mrs. Condrycke's demise may dampen the spirit of the gathering."

"But not by the demise itself?"

The corners of Ludovic's mouth allowed themselves to twitch again. "Mrs. Condrycke was a very old lady, sir. Well into her nineties, I believe, although she exercised a lady's privilege of subtracting a few years. She had been in frail health for some time and uncertain in her temper as a result. Also, she was Squire's mother-in-law, which you will allow may make a difference."

"But her name was Condrycke, too."

"Yes, sir, Squire took the family name when he married her daughter, the late Dorothy Condrycke. There was no male heir at that time, you see. Miss Dorothy was an only child."

"You surprise me. One gets the impression Squire is to the manner born."

"One does indeed, sir. One does not, if I may say so, do anything to contradict that impression."

Rhys nodded. "One wouldn't dream of it. A most affable host, certainly. As a matter of vulgar curiosity and between countrymen, was Graylings his or hers?"

"Graylings was built by the Condryckes, sir, at the peak of the lumber industry in these parts. Lumber was the foundation of the family fortunes."

"And who controls those fortunes now?"

"Under the terms of his marriage agreement, Squire holds life tenure as overall manager of the Condrycke interests."

"Drove a shrewd bargain, did he?"

"Squire is an excellent man of business, sir. His late father-in-law recognized that fact and so did the late Mrs. Condrycke. It was in her interest to let him continue handling affairs at Graylings as he had done so successfully for many years. Even in her more heated moments she has never suggested a desire to change. There would have been no point in his doing anything to hasten her demise, if that is what you are thinking, sir."

"It would be most ill-bred of me to think any such thing," Rhys protested.

"It would be natural enough in your case, sir, I believe."

"Ludovic, you are a credit to your dark and devious race. How did you ever wind up on the Bay Chaleur?"

"It beats a Cardiff coal mine, sir."

It would beat a Cardiff jail, too. If Ludovic could recognize a Mountie in his pajamas, there was probably a reason. Rhys smiled up at the butler in comradeship.

"Is Miss Wadman awake yet, do you know?"

"The young ladies are both asleep, sir, or were when I glanced into their room. Miss Valerie does not take tea in the mornings as a rule."

Ludovic took the empty cup from Rhys. "Speaking as a Welshman and not as a butler, sir, I have seen a great many young ladies in and out of this house, but never one to beat Miss Wadman. She is not also Welsh, by any chance?"

"Her mother was a Hughes, so she must have one foot over the border, at any rate. The Wadmans came out from Derbyshire, I believe, shortly after that unfortunate disagreement among the colonies. They were yeoman farmers and bought part of a Loyalist grant down in Pitcherville."

"The land has remained in the family, sir?"

"Absolutely. Her elder brother is doing an excellent job with the ancestral acres and is raising three fine sons to carry on after him."

"You will be doing the same soon, sir."

Rhys smiled. No doubt Lady Rhys and Janet had that all arranged between them. A boy's best friend was his mother. "Mine is not a hereditary position, Ludovic. Who gets the property after Squire?"

"Strictly speaking, Squire has never had it. Mr. Cyril, as the eldest son, is the legal owner. There is an entail of sorts.

Excuse me, sir. I have enjoyed the unexpected pleasure of your conversation, but I must be getting on with my work. Squire will be down to breakfast any minute now."

"Then I mustn't keep you. I'll be down myself as soon as I get dressed."

"Squire will be glad of your company."

"Ludovic, does he know who I am?"

"He knows you are Sir Emlyn's son and Sir Caradoc's nephew, sir."

"Great-nephew, actually. Thank you, Ludovic. I'll do as much for you sometime."

"I trust I shall not require to avail myself of your services, sir."

They parted on the most amicable of terms and Madoc went to get shaved. So Ludovic knew the Mounties had arrived and Ludovic, unless he was a liar as well as a sometime knave, had not seen fit to apprise his employer of that fact. Rather had not informed his non-employer. It was hard to think of Squire as not being head of Graylings in fact as well as in demeanor and appearance. Rhys wished very much indeed that he knew exactly how the financial arrangements worked at Graylings and what effect Granny's death was going to have on them.

So Cyril was the actual lord of the manor? But did Cyril have any control over the purse strings? And where did Donald, May, and Clara come in? Not to mention Herbert the faithful steward, Lawrence the faithful family lawyer, Ludovic the allegedly faithful old retainer, Valerie the no doubt frequently unfaithful granddaughter, whatever offspring Lawrence and Clara might have, and that pair of May and Herbert's who, from the look of their eyeballs by the end of last evening, had been playing at something other than billiards. With a silent cheer for the marvels of modern electronics, Rhys turned on the shower, reached under the things in his shaving kit, and pulled out a small black box.

"Dick Tracy here," he murmured into the microphone end.

A tinny cackle from the receiver assured him he was on. "Listen, Hercule, I think I've got into something. No, murder for gain, most likely. Looks to me like an old woman done with a pillow, but I've nothing but hunches so far. Everyone's being very polite about it. I'm not asking for help. You'd have a job flying anybody in under these conditions, and at this stage there's not even a case to warrant the effort. I just wanted you to know what's up, and be ready to fly my girl out if things turn sticky. When's the storm supposed to . . . oh, not good, eh? Well, *Joyeux Noël.*"

Down in the States, radio disc jockeys must be dreaming of a white Christmas. Over in Britain, some sweet middle-aged lady with a penchant for gore and a driving lust for an advance royalty check would be pounding out a mystery novel about a house party trapped in a blizzard. This wasn't any real blizzard, not by Canadian standards, but it was pretty thick out there and likely to remain so for a day or two, according to his informant. Fa la la. Rhys buried the midget transistorized two-way radio under his shaving tackle again and went to put some clothes on.

As he was leaving his room, looking especially poetic in the rust-colored heather mixture pullover Janet had so lovingly and laboriously knit for him, the knitter herself came stumbling out into the hall, still wearing her bundle of blue fleece and, no doubt, her pearls and thermal underwear.

"Oh, Madoc, am I late for breakfast?"

"You've missed your morning cuppa, that's all. Ludovic was around with tea a while back. He begged leave to congratulate me on my taste in brides, which I graciously granted. Don't get up yet unless you feel like it. Breakfast will be laid on for at least another hour, I'm sure. And don't prim that stiff upper lip at me or I'll kiss it."

He did anyway. "I'm going down and break a bun with Squire. As to Granny, Ludovic says the drill is that we behave as though nothing has happened."

"Madoc, has something?"

"Not now, darling. I'll see you downstairs. One doesn't make one's own bed, by the way."

Janet looked horrified. "All right if you say so, but I'll never be able to explain to Annabelle."

She gave him a peck on the cheek to ease the pain of parting and went along to the bathroom. Rhys knew he should wish her elsewhere, but how could he when the mere thought of being away from her was too dreadful to admit into consciousness? Anyway, there was no chance of getting her out without putting her to greater risk from the weather than she stood at in the house, and furthermore Ludovic liked her. Whatever had happened to Granny must surely be a family affair. The best protection Rhys could give Janet was to leave it that way, for as long as he could manage.

Playing the role of an undistinguished member of a distinguished family, in love with a young woman as eminently loveworthy as Miss Janet Wadman and not much interested in anything else, should convince any murderer that neither he nor she was a threat. It would involve a lot of hand holding and so forth, but Rhys was not one to shirk so manifest a duty. He had no trouble putting on a shining morning face for Squire.

"Ah, there you are, Madoc. I was wondering if I'd have to eat my porridge alone."

Rhys went to the sideboard and took a plate. "Janet should be along sooner or later. She's getting up now, I believe."

"That's a pleasant surprise. I thought she and Val would chatter half the night and sleep all day."

"Oh, they ragged a bit. Girls will be girls and all that. But Janet was rather done in as she'd mentioned before we went up. By the way, I must tell you that she and I are aware of last night's sad event. We were with Babs and Clara when they found Mrs. Condrycke. It had been a question of whether we were to be introduced, you see. We quite understood why they felt it would be wiser not to spoil the memory of a delightful evening by rousing everyone and spreading the bad news. Janet and I do sympathize most sincerely. If the weather permitted, we'd take our discreet departure, but as we can't do that, please count on us to do whatever will make things easier for you and your family."

"My boy, you mustn't think of leaving. Surely you realize that while we're all naturally grieved, we're not in the least surprised. Considering Granny's age and the state of her health, she could have gone any time these past two years. We'd all bowed to the inevitable some time ago."

Squire put down his porridge spoon and bowed to the inevitable a moment longer, then shook his head and bravely picked up the spoon again. "With the lads home from school and the whole family gathered together for a happy holiday, it would be too cruel to go into mourning for what couldn't have been helped. Clara was quite right in her decision. We must carry on. Granny wouldn't have wanted it any other way, nor do I."

He took a manful scoop of porridge. "Between ourselves, Madoc, life can be damned dreary up here for my daughters during these long winter months. Not that they complain. Wonderful women, both of them, always ready for a prank. I can't help thinking of Queen Alexandra and her children. Did you know that when they got together, those grownup princes and princesses used to romp and play like a crowd of young hobbledehoys? That's the true family spirit, Madoc. That's what I like to see here at Graylings. And damn it," Squire wiped his nose rather savagely on his napkin, "that's what we're going to have this Christmas. I suppose," he added on a more conventionally matter-of-fact note, "it's much the same when your family get together."

Rhys tried to picture his Welsh relatives romping like young hobbledehoys for the edification of his great-uncle and couldn't manage it. They'd more likely be either singing in parts, making up rude rhymes in the ancient bardic tradition, drinking, eating, or exchanging heated views on their pet subjects of religion, music, and sheepdip.

"Oh, you know the Welsh," he murmured. "Our idea of a wild time is reading the juicier bits from the Song of Solomon. This is marvelous bacon, Squire. Home-cured, by any chance?"

"Every bite of it. Herbert's a great hand with the hogs. There'll be roast suckling pig tonight."

"My word, you do your guests proud. Tell me, sir, do we go ahead with the mumming you mentioned?"

"Absolutely. They've all been working on their costumes for months, I shouldn't wonder. Can't deprive them of the chance to show off."

"I'm afraid Janet and I didn't come prepared for a masquerade."

"Oh, we'll rig up something for you. Ah, Janet, there you are now. Looking blithe and bonny, I must say. Did you sleep well?"

"I slept later than I should have, I'm afraid," she replied in a neat evasion. "I do hope I'm not the last one down. Where is everybody?"

"Most of them are still in bed, the wretches. May's out in the kitchen holding a staff conference. Babs is up in the attic hunting out the Christmas trimmings. We always set up the tree on Christmas Eve. Clara came to my room earlier, but I sent her back to bed. I expect she'll be down to help with the tree, though. Perhaps you'd like to lend a hand after breakfast?"

"Of course, I'd love to." Janet hesitated a moment, then came over and gave Squire her hand. "I expect Madoc has told you how sorry we are about your mother-in-law."

"Thank you, my dear, he has. And I've told him we're grateful to have had Granny with us for so many years longer than we could have hoped, and we're not going to spoil our happy time by useless mourning. We've done what little we could for her until the storm lets up and the undertaker can get through, and now we're going straight ahead with our plans as Granny would have wanted us to."

He patted the hand he was still holding. "You know, my dear Janet, back in earlier and happier times when Old England was truly Merrie England, there'd be a Lord of Misrule appointed to preside over the holiday festival, and everybody was expected to obey his royal commands. I've given myself that exalted position, and I hereby command you to step over to that sideboard and choose whatever suits your fancy. Come along and I'll show you what we have."

"No you won't." Janet deftly freed herself from his grasp. "It would be highly improper for the Lord of Misrule to wait on one of his subjects. You stay where you are and look regal. No, Madoc, sit down and finish your eggs before they get cold. I'll be a lady-in-waiting and wait on myself."

Squire chuckled. Madoc had no trouble managing a suitably fatuous laugh.

"Yes, my love. You see, Squire, I'm practicing to become a happily henpecked husband. It's the only way, don't you think?"

"It's the path of least resistance, at any rate. By the way, Janet, you did say you'd been working for Donald?"

"For the firm, at any rate. Not very long, actually. I worked for a while last year, then went home for the summer, and now I'm back and set to quit. He'll be glad to get rid of such a feckless creature, I daresay."

"I find that impossible to believe," Squire replied gallantly. "And you've been sharing an office with Val's friend Roy?"

"Heavens, no. Roy has an office all to himself. I'm only in the typing pool."

"But didn't I hear you say you did his letters?"

"I used to sometimes. Not lately."

"Why not?"

"Because Miss Stewart hasn't assigned me to him, I suppose. Miss Stewart's our department head. She parcels out the work to whichever of us happens to be free, and we just do what she tells us to."

Miss Stewart was as aware as everybody else around the office of the way Roy had chased Janet, then dumped her when she came down with acute appendicitis and spoiled his birthday party. She was much too kind a woman to put Janet in the awkward position of having any further dealings with him. Even though it didn't matter any longer, Janet was not about to explain that to Squire.

"He's a good-looking chap." Was Squire baiting her, by any chance?

"Most of the girls seem to think so." She took her place beside Madoc and picked up her fork. "Roy's well-liked around the office, I should say."

"But you yourself have been too preoccupied to notice, eh? Tell an inquisitive old man how you happened to meet Madoc."

"I tracked her down," Rhys answered for her. "I'd heard about Janet from a mutual acquaintance," Fred Olson, the Pitcherville town marshal, to be specific, "and simply presented myself at her door with my suitcase in my hand. At her brother's door, I should say. I passed myself off as a long-lost relative. Did I not, Cousin Janet?"

"That's exactly what he did, Squire. We spent our first evening together looking at the family album. After that we— well, we got along rather well together and one thing led to another and here we are."

To a Condrycke, that of course was a marvelous joke. "There's one for the books! But you're not really cousins?"

"There is a very distant connection somewhere or other," Madoc replied.

That was undoubtedly true. He'd read somewhere recently that if you could trace anybody's family tree in its entirety back six generations, you'd find that everybody in the world was connected to everybody else now living by the simple laws of mathematical progression. He and Squire might well be related, too, but he didn't think he'd go into that. It wasn't going to hurt Janet's position at Graylings to have it thought she also was related in some degree to Sir Emlyn and Sir Caradoc. She soon would be, in any event.

"Well, look who's here!"

May blew into the room like a gust off the bay. "Everybody getting enough to eat?"

She checked the dishes on the sideboard with a great rattling of lids. "Lawrence can't be down yet. There still appears to be plenty left. Janet, have you tried the finnan haddie? We finnan a great haddie around here. Don't we, Squire?"

"Everything is delicious," Janet assured her. "After that fantastic dinner last night I thought I'd never be hungry again, but I am."

May gave another stir to the smoked fish in its rich cream sauce. "I suppose you've heard about Granny," she said abruptly.

"Yes, and we're terribly sorry. We were just saying so to your father."

"And I told them we're going to carry on as Granny would have wanted us to," said Squire. "Right, my dear?"

"I should hope so."

May did not look to be bowed down by weight of woe. She was wearing a green and yellow striped jersey this morning with, most unfortunately, bright orange stretch-knit trousers. As she was still bending over the sideboard, her husband came in.

"Good God, May, you look like the moon coming over the mountain in that getup," was his fond greeting. "I thought the mumming wasn't till tonight."

He gave her a presumably affectionate skite on the Mount of the Moon and began shoveling eggs and bacon on his plate. "Michel been out to the barn yet?"

"Ages ago. Do you realize what time it is?"

"No, and don't tell me. If this were Vancouver it wouldn't even be sunup yet. Speaking of which, has anybody heard a weather report?"

Rhys had, of course, but he wasn't about to say so.

"Fifine's got that transistor radio blaring in the kitchen as usual," said May. "Or you could ask Aunt Addie. She always knows."

"She was incredible about that fire ship last night," said Janet, "and she told me a couple of other things that," she blushed charmingly, "I would hope might be true."

"You can bank on Aunt Addie," Herbert replied with his mouth full. "Never been wrong yet. Has she, Squire? Oh, Babs. Join the party. We were just discussing Aunt Addie's batting average, as they say down in the States. Ever known her to be wrong about one of her present'ments?"

"Hi, Babs," said May. "Did you find the trimmings?"

"Yes, no problem. They were all stacked just where we left them last year. I've left them stacked at the foot of the attic stairs. You know this stupid arm of mine when it comes to carrying things. Maybe Franny and Winny can bring them down. Hello, Janet, Madoc. I think I'll have another cup of coffee and perhaps just a bite of that finnan haddie if you promise not to tell Donald I sneaked a second breakfast. It's freezing in that attic."

Babs fixed herself a plate and sat down next to Squire. "Getting back to your question, Herbert, I can't say that I ever have known Aunt Addie to miss the mark. You're around her a lot more than I am, of course, so I shouldn't presume to contradict you in any case."

"Tell that to Her Highness, will you? See, May, Babs appreciates me even if you don't."

"I want to hear more about your aunt," Janet insisted. "Can she do it all the time, or just now and then?"

"That depends," said Herbert. "The weather's her big thing. She feels that in her bones, she says. Remarkably sensitive bones Auntie has. Sometimes she'll tell you right to the minute, almost, when a storm's coming and when it's going to stop. But if she doesn't get a feel for it, she won't predict. The fire ship she hears, though don't ask me how. Of course the ship doesn't come along very often, so you couldn't count that as one of her major effects, but it's a whizzer when she brings it off. Weren't you scared stiff last night, Janet?"

"No, why should I have been?" Janet spread the last bit of her marmalade thriftily on her last corner of toast. Trust Janet to make things come out right.

"I was thrilled to pieces, naturally, because I'd never seen a fire ship and always wanted to. The ship was an eerie thing to watch, but I didn't think it was going to sail in through the window and get me or anything. My sister-in-law's mother came from Restigouche County and she said the Phantom Ship usually meant a storm coming. I knew we were in for one anyway because I could smell snow in the air last night when we got out of the helicopter. So I just thought that was why it showed up."

For some reason, all the Condryckes present thought that was a scream. "What have we got here?" cried Herbert. "A second Aunt Addie?"

Janet shrugged. "What's so remarkable about being able to smell snow in the air? I thought everybody could."

"All right, then, tell us when it's going to stop. Within the hour, mind you."

"Four o'clock. But I'm not saying morning or afternoon, or which day." Janet laid down her napkin. "I'll be glad to carry down some of those Christmas trimmings if you'll tell me where to find them, Babs. Squire said I might help to decorate the tree."

"Janet, how sweet of you. Just let me finish this coffee and I'll show you. This house is a jigsaw puzzle to find your way around in."

"It's fascinating. Do you ever give guided tours?"

"You'll get one tonight. We go trooping all through the place scaring the bogles away. That reminds me, we must see about costumes for you two. There's sure to be something in the attic."

"Why don't we tie a couple of eggbeaters to their legs and

let them go as a twin-screw motor?" Herbert suggested suggestively. "Any more tea in the pot, May?"

"Give me some while you're slopping the hogs," said Cyril, joining the breakfast party without ceremony. "Where's Don? Off plotting the murder of the reigning heir, namely me? One step nearer the throne, eh, Squire?"

"Here, have a kidney to stop your mouth."

May slammed a plate down in front of her brother without, for once, trying to make a joke about it. "Donald's helping Baptiste set up the Christmas tree in the Great Hall."

"Energetic of him." Cyril eyed the kidney and took a piece of toast instead. "I hope they get it straight for once."

"How would you know? You're half cockeyed already."

"That's a base canard, which is French for a low duck, in case you're not bilingual, Madoc."

"Thank you. I get most of my language training trying to read the libretti when my mother drags me to hear Dafydd sing."

In point of fact, Rhys was fluent in both city and country French as well as Welsh, Cree, Aleut, and a few more languages, including the officialese in which he was expected to write his reports. However, he preferred to be taken for a nitwit and often was. He'd remarked to Janet last night that the Condryckes must think she was marrying him for his connections, and she'd replied, "Of course I am. Just make sure you stay connected. I like you with all your parts on." An ideal attitude for a policeman's wife. He pushed back his chair and stood up.

"*Avanti,* then, as we say at La Scala. Are there a great many trimmings?"

"Tons. We always have an enormous tree."

Babs put down her empty cup and rose to lead the way. "Anyone who wants to lend a hand is cordially invited. Don't all leap at once."

"Damn the fear of it."

Cyril decided he'd eat the kidney after all. Herbert went to get himself some finnan haddie. Roy appeared, trying not to look the way he no doubt felt, and Janet was glad of an excuse to leave the breakfast room.

CHAPTER 8

Janet had decided to save her white pullover for best and put on a gray-green cardigan with gray flannel pants and a red scarf for a flash of holiday cheer. It was a good thing she had. The boxes were dusty from their year in the attic and there were, as Babs had said, a great many of them.

"How on earth did you get all these things down the attic stairs by yourself?" she asked Babs. "It must have taken ages. Why didn't you wait and let us lug them the whole way down?"

"Oh, I didn't mind. That's my way of working off a few calories so I can pig it later with a clear conscience. You young things don't have to worry but, as I keep telling Val, wait till you get to be my age."

Babs was in fact looking svelte and trim with a bright print smock over her sleek black trousers and a black pullover in the cowl-necked style she favored. It looked like real cashmere and no doubt was. Babs couldn't be wearing mourning for Granny because one didn't in the country. Black cashmere was simply the sort of thing she'd wear.

It was interesting to see how differently the Condryckes wore the same sorts of clothes. Clara was safely tasteful, May was flamboyant, Val a conformist in her own way though she'd have raised the roof if anybody said so. Babs was the one with a real sense of style.

She had also the instincts of a good general. Roy hadn't dawdled over breakfast. Perhaps because he was trying to demonstrate what an up-and-coming young man he was, he bustled into the Great Hall to help with the tree. To Janet's dismay, Babs delegated him to help carry down ornaments while Madoc, as the lightest and most agile man present, was sent up the tall wooden stepladder to hang spun-glass frivolities on the topmost branches. That left Janet and Roy to make the last trip to the foot of the attic stairs together. It worked out pretty much as Janet expected.

"Look, Janet," Roy began as soon as they were up on the top floor out of everyone else's earshot, "I know what you must think of me."

"Then there's no point in discussing it, is there?" she replied. "Can you manage that last boxful? Be careful with it. Babs says some of these ornaments are almost a hundred years old and I daresay they're worth a young fortune."

"Do you have to be that way?"

"I'm the way I am, Roy. Those who don't like my manners will just have to lump 'em. You and I happen by coincidence to be guests of the Condryckes. We have a duty to be civil as long as we're under their roof, so let's do the best we can and leave it at that, eh?"

"But I don't want to leave it at that," he protested, trying to take her hand. "Janet, I made a terrible mistake about you."

"Then don't make another. For instance, don't fool yourself into thinking my folks must have more money than you thought they did just because I've happened to get myself involved with a prominent family. I'm no better catch now than I was eight months ago. Madoc knows all about me, he's visited my folks, he's marrying me for the simple reason that he wants to, and don't for one second think he's not a better man than you are or that I haven't brains enough to know it. I don't have what you're looking for, Roy, and wouldn't give it to you if I did, so quit trying to tickle your vanity at my expense. And furthermore you're skating on thin ice with Val Condrycke because you were dumb enough to get drunk last night, so paste that pretty smile back on your face and go flash it where it will do you some good. Now are you going to carry that last box, or shall I?"

"Oh, permit me, your ladyship."

It wasn't much of an effort, but maybe it made Roy feel a little better. Janet couldn't have cared less one way or the other. She went on ahead, relieved to have got the inevitable confrontation over with and concerned only not to drop the fragile ornaments.

Catching a glimpse of Granny's bedroom door as they twisted around a corner, she noticed somebody had affixed a black bow and a spray of artificial lilacs to it. That was an understandable way to show respect for the dead, she supposed, especially since nothing else could be done until the storm was over and the undertaker arrived. But the bow was too large, the flowers too obviously plastic, and the whole effect too much like one of Herbert's practical jokes for her taste.

Not, Janet reminded herself, that it was any of her business. Anyway, down in the Great Hall it was easy enough to forget that overdone tribute to an old woman nobody appeared to be mourning. Madoc's detective instinct must have alerted him to what had happened up by the attic stairs, for he cocked an eyebrow and brushed his fingertips against the inside of her wrist as she reached to hand him up a bauble in the shape of an angel flying a hot-air balloon. She smiled back and blew a kiss to the top of the ladder.

The tree was a balsam fir so tall that not even the biggest of the Condryckes could have reached the topmost branches without something to stand on. Back home, Bert and the kids and an assortment of uncles and cousins would be out in the woodlot by now cutting a tree about a quarter the size of this one, which would still have to be trimmed down when they got it home in order to fit inside the modest farmhouse. Annabelle and her sister-in-law and the Lord knew how many more would be in the kitchen, stirring and baking, drinking cup after cup of tea, chattering nineteen to the dozen.

There'd be more affection than wit in their conversation and nobody would be playing a practical joke on anybody unless one of the kids took a notion to stuff a handful of snow down somebody else's neck and get his own face washed in retaliation. Janet wasn't homesick, but she did feel most profoundly blessed to have been born a Wadman instead of a Condrycke. Or instead of a Rhys for that matter, because if she'd been Madoc's sister she couldn't very well become his wife without causing talk. She gave her betrothed such a look of adoration that he almost fell off the ladder.

By then Val had made her appearance and Roy was lavishing his attentions on her to show Janet what she'd been fool enough to pass up. Val had on a different pair of designer jeans today, a pair of boots with unimaginably high heels, and another oversized pullover. It had been handknit in Italy of shocking pink mohair by somebody who must have suffered a great many sneezing fits before it was done. Franny and Winny poked their noses into the Great Hall just long enough to sneer at the tree-trimming party and mutter that they were going to play billiards.

"They're going through a phase," Babs said indulgently to Clara.

Janet thought Bert would have handled the phase by setting the pair to work at a two-handed saw till they'd emerged from their sulks with a few armloads of stove wood to show for it, but apparently that wasn't how things were done among the upper crust. She'd better clarify that point with Madoc before they started having young ones of their own.

Squire, Lawrence, and Herbert were having some sort of conference in the library, no doubt as a result of Granny's death and whatever family business it would entail. Cyril was with them but Donald, for some reason, was not. Janet would have thought the one businessman among them would be the first to sit in at such a meeting.

Val evidently thought so, too, for she asked him, "Daddy, how come you're not in there with Squire and the rest?"

Donald laughed indulgently. "Because I'm here keeping a fatherly eye on my beautiful daughter. Val, you should know by now that my responsibility is to represent the family interests down in Saint John. I couldn't manage both that and Graylings. Why should I? Squire has Herbert, Lawrence, and Cyril to help him. That's not a spider on your back, by any chance?"

"Ugh! One of Uncle Herb's little nasties, I suppose."

Val squirmed and Roy leaped to be gallant. Madoc Rhys sat up on his ladder wondering why Donald Condrycke had chosen that particular moment to tangle a fake spider in his daughter's expensive mohair.

The tree took a long time to finish, even with so many working at the decorating. There were no lights, since there'd have been nowhere to plug in electric ones and candles were out of the question.

"Too dangerous," Donald explained. "We're miles from a fire station here, as you must realize. Anyway, the tree's so big that by the time we'd got the last one lit the first would be burned down. We do cheat a bit and hide a battery lantern behind the trunk so we can enjoy it at night. At least I presume we do. Is that in the drill this year, Clara?"

"It is if we can find some extra batteries. May was fussing that we seem to be running short, for some reason. Of course we do use an awful lot of them, one way and another, around here."

"It would be so nice if Squire would get on with the general electrification," Babs sighed.

"I couldn't agree more," said Clara, "but Lawrence claims the cost would be prohibitive and Cyril objects on general principles. You know Cy and his sense of history."

Janet looked rather surprised, though she was too well bred to say anything. She must be thinking Squire was a remarkably benevolent tyrant if he put up with so much inconvenience in deference to his son's sense of history. Rhys thought it might be as well for her to go on thinking so.

This question of how much to tell your wife was going to be a sticker. Some of his colleagues had trouble with it, he knew. Rhys had never understood why, but then he'd never before loved a woman enough to want to share everything with her and at the same time protect her from any possible mischance. He didn't know what he was trying to shield Janet from, he only knew that an old woman who'd probably have died soon anyway was now murdered for no apparent reason, and that things were not what they seemed at Graylings. That, in his experience, was enough to make the boldest wary. He hung the last trimming, agreed that the tree was indeed a thing of beauty, and asked where he should put the ladder.

"Better let me. It looks heavy."

That was Janet's ex-boyfriend, flexing his muscles at the expense of this puny Welshman she'd been silly enough to settle for. Let him. The poor chap was having a bad morning. Val wasn't giving him much time and clearly he'd had some sort of set-to with Janet upstairs, in which he'd come off a poor second. Rhys wasn't about to shed any tears over that.

One could see why a girl fresh off the farm would have fallen for a good-looker like Roy. He must be a practiced charmer since he'd also been able to attract so experienced a campaigner as Val evidently was. Val had been one of Dafydd's dates, and Dafydd had his own code of ethics, such as it was. Deflowering virgins was not on the list, assuming he'd ever met one.

Lady Rhys must have told Dafydd and the rest of the family about Janet by now, and they must be thinking Mother was making her up. Women like Janet Wadman didn't exist. If they did, why should they want to marry clods like Madoc who couldn't even read music? Madoc was damned if he'd hold up his wedding for Dafydd. It galled him to think that if Lady Rhys hadn't been so officious about getting them invited to Graylings, he and his Jenny could be hunting up a justice of the peace right now instead of standing around with pitch on their fingers and apprehension in their hearts wondering which of their genial hosts and/or hostesses had bumped off dear old Granny.

This might even turn out to be a classic case of the butler done it. Ludovic was a capable man, and a man who could well be working his own mysterious courses at Graylings. Criminal record or not, he needn't bury himself in so desolate a post unless he was (a) getting paid a great deal more for his services than he'd get elsewhere; (b) in love with the cook; or (c) running a little something on the side.

They'd only Ludovic's word for it that Granny had been alive before they went in to dinner. Squire had sent the butler up alone to see why the old lady hadn't appeared in the Great Hall and the man had come back with that ludicrous report of the missing teeth, the sort of absurdity the Condryckes would be delighted to accept without bothering to check its veracity. The teeth had shown up in the silliest place possible as soon as dinner was over and there could be no question of Granny's coming down, but who was to say how long the bear had been wearing them?

After dinner when May had decided on coffee in the library, it had been Ludovic who'd gone ahead to mend the fire and fetch the tray. He wouldn't have required more than a second to take the teeth out of his pocket and stick them in the bear's mouth. He'd know the family's only reactions would be to accuse each other and regret that they themselves hadn't thought of pinching the teeth first.

Ludovic had made a second trip with that pitcher of wassail, and what of that? He could have drunk the stuff himself, or poured it down the bathroom sink, or given it to Granny for purposes of anesthesia and then done his dirty work. An autopsy would show whether in fact Mrs. Condrycke had drunk the wassail, but would it be possible to have an autopsy performed?

There must be a doctor somewhere nearby who'd been looking after her. The odds were he'd sign a certificate without demur and why shouldn't he when it was a case of an old woman who, according to Squire, had been more or less written off some time ago? Doctors didn't create scandals among patients like the Condryckes if they could help it.

Come to think of it, Squire hadn't even mentioned calling in the doctor to view the remains although he had sent for the undertaker. Was that because he didn't know the proper steps to take or because he took it for granted there'd be no hitch in the formalities?

Janet was twisting a long strand of tinsel rope around the base of the tree. She stopped and looked up at Babs. "I just thought of a costume. May I use some of this?"

"Certainly, take all you like. Will you need anything else?"

"No, except—excuse me a moment." She went over and whispered to Madoc.

He nodded in mild surprise. "As a matter of fact, yes. How did you know?"

"Because you never got a chance to."

He laughed and gave her a hug. "Ah, Jenny love, you're the girl for me."

"She is." Aunt Adelaide had materialized again without seeming to have entered the room. "I told her that last night. I told her not to let anybody talk her out of it. Somebody already has but it didn't work. She didn't know who you were, did she? Not till your mother told her. Your mother was right to give her the ring, so you needn't worry about Janet's having it. You have been worrying, haven't you?"

"Well, a little," Rhys admitted. "As I told Squire, I did more or less walk in on Janet and say, 'My name is Rhys, would you care to share it?' It was in fact my mother who filled her in on the family situation, and that wasn't till yesterday. Remember, Jenny love?"

"How could I forget? I called her Mrs. Rhys and almost died of mortification when she raised her eyebrows and said, 'Madoc, you idiot, didn't you *explain?*'"

Janet giggled at the recollection. "I thought Madoc was

just another lost sheep on the mountain like me. The last time we were up home, he was lecturing my brother Bert about the best way to build a pigpen. I told Lady Rhys that and she laughed so hard I thought we'd have to give her first aid."

Those Condryckes present obliged by laughing also, but less heartily than was their wont. "And then she went ahead and gave you her diamond?" Val said, as if she didn't believe a word of it.

"It was the least she could do," Madoc confirmed. "Mother was the one who proposed to Janet. Not that I hadn't meant to, you understand, but she got hers in first. Mother's rather like that. She had to catch a plane to London and she didn't want to miss the engagement party, so she hauled off one of her own rings and there we were. That's the one Janet has on now. It belonged to my great-grandmother, I think. Wasn't that what Mother said, darling?"

"Yes, and she'd always intended to give it to whichever of her children got engaged first or said she did."

"Oh, Mother wouldn't say a thing like that unless she meant it. I wanted to buy Janet a new one yesterday but she dug in her little heels and wouldn't let me, so we're going to take the money and build a better pigpen instead. Anyway, I'm glad to have your certificate of approval, Miss Adelaide, and particularly grateful you've warned Jenny not to get talked out of marrying me. Mother would have fits if she backed off now. How do you know these things?"

"I only tell what I see," said the old woman. "I never know what's coming and sometimes I don't see things you'd think I ought to. Like poor Rosa, for instance. I could have sworn she was meant to outlive me. Well, the ship will be coming for me next, I shouldn't wonder. You young things have your fun while you can. I think I'll go back to Rosa for a while."

CHAPTER 9

Babs and Clara exchanged looks. "Oh, dear," Clara sighed. "I only hope she doesn't go spreading doom and gloom in front of Squire."

"She'll probably stay upstairs a good bit today," Babs consoled her sister-in-law. "I suppose Aunt Addie is taking Granny's death harder than the rest of us. At her age, one would tend to get that 'me next' feeling."

Donald made an odd little noise. "You know, I'd quite forgotten Granny's name was Rosa. Clara, do you remember the time Cyril said, 'Every Rosa has its thorns,' and she hit him with her cane?"

"Must have been over the head," said May, who'd come in just in time to hear her brother's boyhood reminiscence. "Where was I, I wonder?"

"At school, most likely. That wasn't too long after Mother died, when Clara and I still had the governess, I forget which one. We did go through them rather fast. Either they couldn't stand Graylings or we couldn't stand them."

"And Cyril had been sent home again, I suppose, because his headmaster couldn't stand him," Clara added rather nastily. "What's this costume you're cooking up, Janet?"

"Nothing much, really. It's just a silly idea I had."

"The sillier the better," May assured her. "Wait till you see Herbert and the boys and me! Speaking of the menfolks, how long do you suppose they're going to keep nattering in there? Fifine's coming to a slow boil about lunch and my tongue's hanging out for a drink."

"So is Cyril's, I'm sure." Clara really was in a mood today.

"But you know what Lawrence is like once he gets started on the party of the first part and the party of the second part. Squire must be in a proper swivet by now."

"Drag him under the mistletoe and we'll elect Janet to kiss him out of it," May advised.

"Oh, my God," cried Babs. "We've forgotten to hang up the kissing ball. Where is it, quick?"

A frantic scurrying ensued. At last May unearthed a handsome ball of boxwood and mistletoe tied with red velvet ribbons that Clara took well-deserved credit for having arranged. Roy was sent back to get the ladder he'd just taken away and a hot dispute over where to hang the ball this year was in progress when the meeting at last broke up.

If Squire was in a swivet, he didn't show it. He looked the embodiment of Christmas Present as he stood with a glass of Rainwater Madeira in his hand directing the placement of the kissing ball. When it was hung to his satisfaction, everybody cheered and drank one of the toasts the Condryckes were so addicted to. Roy had got the ladder nicely folded and was about to take it to the woodshed once more when Cyril stopped him.

"Wait a minute. I think the ball would look better in the doorway."

"You know what happened the last time we did that," May objected. "Somebody was always reaching up with the poker or something and batting it off the hook."

"Yes, Granny kept hitting it with her cane. I think we should hang the mistletoe there in memory of Granny."

Cyril's eyes were glittering. He appeared to be oddly strung up. Rhys wondered if something had happened at that meeting or whether Cyril was already one over the eight.

Squire didn't like this. For a moment it looked as if Cyril was about to get a blasting. Then the father got his benignity back.

"Of course, Cyril, if it's important to you. Roy, would you mind?"

Roy was clearly beginning to mind, but there wasn't much he could do except pretend he didn't. He climbed back up and retrieved the ball he'd spent so much time getting arranged to everybody's satisfaction. Cyril then fussed around for quite a while deciding precisely where in the doorway Roy should hang the ball. As soon as it was placed and the ladder taken away, he jumped up, took a mighty swipe, and sent the kissing ball hurtling across the room almost into the Christmas tree.

"Ha! Score one for my side. Stick it back up there, Roy. How about a drink, Herb?"

"How about lunch?" May got her brother in a neat armlock. "Everything's on the table and you two will be under it if you don't quit swilling and get something into your stomachs. Leave the ladder, Roy, in case Cyril changes his mind again. Val, run up and tell Aunt Addie we're sitting down now, will you? Ask her if she's coming or if she'd rather have something on a tray."

"Dangerous things, trays," said Cyril. He must surely be drunk. "Granny had one, and look what happened to her."

All the Condryckes began talking about other things and surging toward the dining room. Herbert put a toy lizard down Clara's back. She screamed in a gratifying way, then managed to divert Cyril's attention by putting the lizard in the drink he was still carrying.

"Haven't seen one of these in my glass for quite a while."

He swung the rubber toy around by its tail and spun it neatly into the midst of a handsome centerpiece of Christmas greens Babs had arranged for the table. "Down with the demon rum. Come on, Janet, sit by me and we'll play kneesies."

"No you won't."

Madoc grabbed his intended and placed her firmly between himself and Lawrence. "One false move and I'll sue you for alienation of affections. Lawrence will handle the case, I'm sure. Anyway, Janet's already received the gypsy's warning about being lured away by richer and handsomer men. Your aunt says she's stuck with me for keeps."

"Aunt Addie had better watch out or I'll send the Phantom Ship after her. All right, Janet, you had your chance and you muffed it."

Cyril picked up his wine glass and waved it over his head. "Come, Ludo, fill the flowing bowl until it doth run over. For tonight we'll merry, merry be, tomorrow we'll be sober. You will, that is. I shan't. Drink, drink, drink to the eyes are— whatever eyes are."

"Bloodshot, in your case," said his sister. "Shut up and eat."

"What's all this garbage about getting me to eat? Something up your sleeve, Maysie? A pinch of arsenic, for instance? I think I'm going to get myself a taster. How about it, Lawrence?"

"Yeah, Uncle Lawrence would make a good taster."

That was Winny, and it was virtually the only remark Rhys had heard him utter so far. His brother poked him in the ribs and they got into a sit-down boxing match which their father ordered them to stop.

"Let them alone," said Squire indulgently. "Boys will be boys."

"These two won't be for much longer unless they straighten up and fly right," Cyril contradicted his father. "Do you two care to start acting like young gentlemen for a change, or would you rather start walking to Dalhousie?"

"Who's going to make us?" Franny demanded, ignoring his own father's glare.

"He who has been sucker enough to foot your bills up till about two seconds ago," Cyril replied. "Shape up or ship out, lads. The gravy train is no longer running. Ludovic, my glass."

"Cyril, I don't think you fully understood the ramifications of what we've been discussing," Lawrence began. "In point of fact, you do not . . ."

"In point of fact, I do, my dear brother-in-law. If you don't agree, I'm sure I can find myself a lawyer who does."

"Herbert, where do we keep the Mickey Finns?" said May. "All right, Cyril, your nephews will now kiss the hem of your garment in abject apology. Or would you prefer to have them wait till they've finished eating, in case of gravy stains? Ludovic, for goodness' sake keep 'em coming till he's drunk himself either sociable or insensible, which in Cyril's case would be synonymous. Right, you old soak?"

She ruffled her brother's hair affectionately and squawked her parrot at him. Cyril gave her a wobbly nod.

"Good effort, May. I'll unravel your name from the scarf I'm knitting."

"Thank you, brother dear. Anyone for ham? Better grab it quick before Uncle Cyril says you can't have any more."

"Oh, Uncle Cyril wouldn't begrudge little Vallie a weentsy slice."

His niece gave him a smile that would have been more effective if Uncle Cyril hadn't had his eyes closed. He was undoubtedly at the passing-out stage by now. Everybody was eager to make it known they realized he was and that allowances must be made accordingly.

"I'm afraid Cyril feels the loss of his grandmother terribly," Babs murmured to Madoc, who happened to have her on the side where Janet wasn't. "People do show odd reactions to stress sometimes, don't they."

Rhys agreed that they did and expressed the opinion that Cyril would feel better after he'd had a little nap. In fact he thought Cyril was feeling pretty rosy already. It would be interesting to find out what had gone on behind that library door this morning. Thanks to Ludovic's attack of confidentiality, he thought he could guess. Squire might have brought up his sons in the not unnatural misapprehension that their father was the actual as well as the acting head of Graylings. Perhaps Cyril had only this morning learned, as a result of whatever legal formalities Granny's death had made necessary, that he himself was the true and lawful heir. Whether in fact he had the right to turn off his kith and kin at will was debatable, but considering that Cyril must be well over fifty years old and probably missing on a cylinder or two from chronic alcoholism, one could understand why he might now be feeling vindictive and inclined to throw his weight about.

Janet touched Madoc's arm. "Do you suppose we could borrow some snowshoes and get out for a little while?" she murmured. "It's not snowing all that hard right now and I'd love a breath of fresh air."

"Good idea, love. So should I."

Under the circumstances, it might be tactful of them to make themselves scarce for a while. They could stay close to the house. Then there'd be no danger of losing themselves even if the snow did come on heavily all of a sudden. He passed on Janet's request to Babs, who was all for it.

"There are lots of skis and snowshoes in the woodshed. You just go down the long hall and through the door at the end. All the outbuildings are connected by covered sheds so they can be got at without going outdoors, winters being what they are up here. If you get cold, just come in any door you can find and walk through. There should be people around who could set you straight if you get lost in the barns, except that most of them can't speak English, or won't."

"That's all right, Janet and I can make ourselves understood in French if we have to."

In fact Janet was almost as fluent as Madoc, thanks to Annabelle and her many relatives. Rhys quite liked his future sister-in-law and all the Duprees he'd met so far. It was a damned shame they hadn't taken their chances on Marion Emery's hospitality and gone to meet brother Pierre and his tribe instead of the Condryckes. He'd a far sight rather be sitting at the kitchen table with Bert right now having a modest tot of rum than drinking this excellent claret and wondering what new disaster was going to strike next.

At any rate, now that Cyril was peacefully slumbering with

his chin propped on May's shoulder, Squire was back in charge and misrule happily restored. Herbert was showing Val how to make castanets out of two spoons. Roy was laughing a good deal at her efforts so that everybody could see what nice, white teeth he had. Clara was telling a screamingly funny story about some local club she belonged to. At least there was a good deal of screaming, so it must be funny.

Clara had a malicious sense of humor for one who dressed in such demurely subdued taste. Rhys could picture her at the club meeting, perhaps wearing the same brown and beige ensemble she had on now, smiling politely and sipping her tea while she stored up her fellow members' little follies for her family's amusement.

She and Lawrence lived in one of the neighboring towns, it appeared, but spent most of their weekends at Graylings now that their own young had flown the nest. There was a married daughter down in the States, and a son making his fortune in the oil fields out around Banff. Neither of them could get home for the holidays, for reasons their parents managed to extract a fair amount of humor out of.

Clara must have started a good deal earlier than her sister to raise her family. She was evidently Squire's baby, and May next oldest to Cyril. The mother having died young, May had stepped into a quasi-maternal role, as witness her present solicitude for the plastered Cyril. He didn't know how lucky he was. A sister like Gwen would have left him to drown in the gravy after the way he'd been acting before he committed the final breach of passing out at the luncheon table.

May had no doubt been gently discouraged by Squire from setting out to seek her fortune. He couldn't have remarried himself so long as Granny was alive without jeopardizing his position at Graylings, and that boundless energy of his daughter's must come in handy around a place this size. May did appear to be a competent housekeeper and a bit of a diplomat in spite of her clothes and her voice. That hoydenish manner might well be an outlet for frustration, or else a valiant though nerve-wracking way of fighting back at the cold and the solitude. There were many kinds of courage, and human personalities could be a very mixed bag.

Finding a husband couldn't have been any cinch for May. Had Herbert come here to be steward, as Squire so grandly called him, and then fallen in love with the stay-at-home eldest daughter? Or had the job been used as bait to lure and keep him here? And was it in truth May he cared for, or a soft berth on a lavishly run estate? Herbert got paid well, no doubt, for whatever services he rendered. Squire could afford to be generous, since it was not his own substance he was dispensing. Perhaps that was why Cyril had started twisting the knife so viciously. It must have been a shock to learn he'd spent his lifetime drinking up his own estate instead of his father's. Rhys pushed back his chair and politely declined the offer of a cigar in the library.

"I have to take the little woman for an airing. Janet and I thought we'd put on snowshoes and stroll around the house. We still haven't seen what Graylings looks like from the outside, you know."

"So you haven't. By the way, I've been meaning to ask whether you went so far as to charter that helicopter just to come up here. We'd be terribly honored if you did," said Squire.

"No, I'm afraid we only hitched a lift with a friend," Rhys confessed. "He's going to pick us up, by the way, in case you've been wondering how we're to get back."

"Not too soon, I hope?"

"Actually I'm not quite sure. Either tomorrow afternoon or the morning after, I believe, if that fits into your plans. It will depend a bit on the weather, of course."

"Please feel free to stay as long as you like. We do have an emergency CB radio if you want to get a message through and the telephone lines aren't working."

"I thought you might. This place is fantastically well equipped."

"Has to be. We never know when or for how long we'll be snowed in, being off the main track as we are."

"But you have your own plow?"

"It's not up to heavy roadwork. We use it mostly to keep the drives open and the barns clear. You and Janet would do better to stick to the plowed areas. That way you can't get lost."

"I expect we shan't stay out long in any case. Come on, love, let's get changed. Anyone care to join the party?"

CHAPTER 10

Nobody took Madoc up on his invitation. That suited him and Janet just fine. They put on the heavy clothes they'd traveled in, and found the woodshed where every kind of snowshoes from wide bearpaws to long, slim racing types were hanging. Madoc chose the reliable bearpaws from force of habit, while Janet picked out a pair that looked like her oldest nephew's because those were the ones she usually borrowed.

It was not paralyzingly cold out. There was no wind to speak of, so the snow didn't drive into their faces like ice-coated bullets. By local standards, this might have been considered a fairly agreeable day. Madoc gave Janet a hand up over the drifts, and they started their walk.

"Let's keep near the house and just circle around it," Madoc suggested. "Storms off the water can be tricky. I've a hunch we shouldn't stray far."

"I was thinking the same thing." Janet hadn't made any move to withdraw her mitten from his, as why should she? "It will be getting dark soon anyway, and I've got to do something about our costumes for tonight."

"Jenny, you're not expecting me to make an ass of myself?"

"No, darling. I thought you could wear your dinner jacket and carry a little stick for a baton, and go as your father. I'll make myself a tinsel crown and pretend I'm the Queen Mum."

"Leave it to you!"

He laughed and managed to kiss her though snowshoes are

not well adapted to togetherness. "Shentlemen in the basses, a little more glissando in the catenzass, if you pleass."

"Is that how your father talks, like a real Welshman?"

"Dearest, he is a real Welshman."

"And which are you?"

"I'm Canadian. The only one in the family, as a matter of fact. Dafydd and Gwen were both born in London."

"But I thought Dafydd was in his thirties and Gwendolyn about my age."

"That's right. Gwennie's only twenty-two. An infant, like you."

Madoc would be twenty-eight next month. High time for a man to settle down and start a family of his own. "Father's always had to shunt back and forth a good deal. He'd park us in Wales with his uncle when he was on tour and we weren't off at school or at the house in Winnipeg, so I grew up almost as Welsh as the rest. Uncle Caradoc always made a thing of having Welsh spoken in his home."

"Shall I have to learn?"

"You'll pick up a few words here and there, I expect. It's not a bad idea. One never knows when it will come in handy."

"I should imagine it might." Janet shielded her face with her free mitten, for they were now heading into the storm. "Ludovic's Welsh, isn't he?"

"How did you know?"

"Feminine intuition. Actually, you and he look to me as if you have some kind of *rapport*, as Mama Dupree would say. I couldn't think what else it might be unless he's somebody you arrested once."

"And why would I arrest him?"

"I don't know, but there must be some reason why he sticks himself off up here at Graylings, mustn't there?"

"I'm inclined to think so, but I don't intend to ask. Ludovic and I are indeed *en rapport*, and I'd like us to stay that way until I can get you safely out of this."

"Then there is something funny going on." Janet stated it

as a fact, not a question. "What's got into Cyril, do you know? He wasn't like that last night. Has it anything to do with his grandmother's dying?"

"I shouldn't be surprised. Ludovic and I had a pleasant little conversation this morning when he brought up the tea. I'd thought I detected a familiar accent, so I spoke to him in Welsh. That melted the ice. He hadn't heard it spoken since he was a babe on his grandfather's knee. Pinching the old man's watch and chain, no doubt. Anyway, the gist is that Squire is not in fact the squire. The Condryckes, who owned Graylings and God knows what else, had no male heir so he took their name when he married their only daughter. He apparently has some kind of lifetime curacy, but actual ownership of Graylings passed directly to Cyril as the eldest living genuine Condrycke. I think what may have happened is that Cyril didn't quite realize the true position until this morning, when he had to be told for some legal reason or other resulting from the old lady's death."

"My word! No wonder Squire calls himself Lord of Misrule. That's what he's been all along."

"I don't have all the facts, but as far as I could make out what he's been doing is perfectly legitimate," Madoc reminded her. "The grandmother was quite content to have Squire manage the property. Ludovic says he's a capable man of business and has done a first-class job, which certainly appears to be the case. Whether Cyril could have done as well is anybody's guess."

"He'd have dribbled it all away in five years' time is my guess," said Janet. "Cyril reminds me of my Aunt Prudence's oldest son Renny. She had five and the rest all turned out well enough, but Renny's a weak fish and always has been. They owned a general store. It was doing fine till Uncle Abner died and Renny took over. He liked being boss, but he didn't care much for work and he couldn't handle responsibility. The store would have gone out of business if the brothers hadn't chipped in to buy him out. Now he's run through what they gave him and goes whining around after an allowance because he claims they tricked him out of his birthright. I don't blame Squire. If he'd been fool enough to step aside, none of them would have a roof over their heads by now. And they won't much longer if Cyril starts throwing his weight around, you mark my words."

"Consider them duly marked. Jenny, are you enjoying this?"

"Well, I'm finding it interesting, in a way," she replied. "I can't say it's what I expected, but I'm learning some things I probably needed to know. And Graylings really is a work of art in its way, wouldn't you think? A little overworked in spots, but worth coming to see."

"It's that and then some," Madoc agreed, measuring the expanses of crenellated and convoluted clapboard with a snow-filled eye. "One would hate to see it go down the drain like your Uncle Abner's store, so let's hope Cyril starts behaving himself. He and everyone else."

Rhys did wish he could get some kind of line on who was responsible for that wisp of wassail-soaked hair still in his bathrobe pocket. Could Granny's death by any chance have been intended to provoke Cyril into acting up and trying to unseat Squire? Jenny was quite right about Cyril's inability to run Graylings or anything else, in his judgment. The odds were he wouldn't be all that interested in trying to do so. He'd be more apt to make the odd feint of giving instructions and in fact leave everything to Herbert, the faithful steward who was also a congenial drinking buddy and had a merry way with trick lizards.

And faithful Herbert was married to motherly May who'd been unraveled from the scarf Cyril Defarge was knitting because she knew so well how to manage her bibulous brother. And May was a woman with plenty of life in her and no lack of common sense. May might like a break from the role she'd been thrust into, or jumped into without seeing it was a trap, after she'd left the school where she'd no doubt captained the field hockey team and put fake lizards in other girls' beds.

May also had a couple of young sons who were riding for a long fall if they didn't get themselves straightened out soon. There wasn't much May could do about the boys as long as she was committed to keeping the home fires burning and dutifully shipping Franny and Winny off to the boarding school of Squire's choice.

She might or might not realize what was happening to her offspring. If she didn't, she must be more unaware, or more swamped with other duties, than would seem possible. If she did, either she'd already worked off her maternal urges on her siblings or else there was a desperate woman as well as a capable actress stuffed into those impossible orange pants. He did wish he dared thrash out this whole business with Janet. How the hell did the other chaps handle this problem with their wives?

"What did you mean about learning things you needed to know?" he asked cautiously.

"It's just that I realized from the beginning I'd have to rub up against all sorts of people and situations after we were married, so I thought I'd better look for chances to practice. That was why I went back to Saint John."

She laughed. "Oh, dear, I shouldn't have admitted that. I'd only known you about three weeks then, hadn't I?"

"Darling, you don't mean you'd already decided?"

"I don't know that I ever decided, exactly. Madoc, do you remember that night in Pitcherville, when we walked down to the pond to see the fireflies?"

"How could I forget?" He squeezed her mitten. "I've wondered ever since why I didn't propose to you right then and get it over with."

"Liar. You'd only met me the day before and you didn't know but what you'd have to arrest me for murder."

"Granted, but I was hopelessly stuck on you already. It was a very awkward situation."

"I don't remember it as awkward at all. Everything had been so awful, and I was feeling so terrible about losing Mrs. Treadway and finding Dr. Druffitt the way I did, and worried sick about what might happen next, and that scalded hand was killing me and then all of a sudden there you were and it wasn't awful any more. I just couldn't bear to think you'd ever go away. And I could tell you . . . you did seem to like my pie awfully well. So I couldn't help thinking what it would be like."

"Then why didn't you come to Fredericton instead of Saint John?" Rhys asked rather angrily, thinking of all the nights he'd spent alone in his bachelor apartment cursing the distance between him and Janet.

"Then you wouldn't have had the fun of chasing me," she told him. "Anyway, I'd made a fool of myself over a man once before and I wasn't about to get stung twice. But when you sent me that box of chocolates with the Mountie on the lid, and all those silly postcards my landlady had such fun reading, I began to think maybe you meant it and I'd better study up a little. I did think of going down to the jail and chatting with a few crooks, but that seemed a bit much so I decided I'd concentrate on making the most of whatever opportunities came along. That's what I'm doing now. How far do you think we've come?"

"Getting tired?"

"This is an awfully thick storm, and the snow's so wet it's clumping on my snowshoes. I'll bet they weigh thirty pounds apiece by now."

"Then we'd better go in. They're probably wondering about us anyway."

"You mean wondering what we're up to out in one of those barns somewhere," Janet panted. "Do you suppose there's a door anywhere along here?"

"Bound to be. Ah yes. They don't call me detective for nothing. Damn, it's locked."

"What are we going to do?" Janet was beginning to feel a

bit panicky. This had been a foolish expedition in such a storm. Madoc wouldn't have come if she hadn't made him. If they froze to death—by the time she'd got that far in her self-recriminations, Madoc had the lock neatly jimmied and they were inside.

They shook themselves as dry as they could and walked down the hallway carrying their snowshoes. This was a part of Graylings they'd never been in before. They had no idea where they were headed until a faint odor as of burning herbs reached their nostrils.

"My detective instinct tells me this is the billiard room," Rhys murmured. "The lads are amusing themselves in their own quiet way."

"I had a hunch they were shooting something besides pool," Janet replied with a degree of sophistication that amazed her beloved. "Do you think their parents know?"

"They may prefer not to. Sh-h!"

Rhys paused to engage in an activity that would have been unthinkable according to Sir Emlyn's definition of a shentle-man. Franny and Winny were in conference.

"So what does it mean, eh? Does it mean we're going to get thrown out on our ears because Uncle Cyril's got all the loot, eh, or does it mean we don't go back to school and get stuck back here for the rest of our lives, eh? What I mean is, what does it mean? I thought Squire owned everything and Dad had to work here because Mum was Squire's mother—I mean Squire was Mum's—I mean, you know what I mean. But now Uncle Cyril says it's his and what I mean is, what does it mean? Eh?"

"You're stoned."

The other burst into giggles and so did the one who'd been wondering what it meant. After that they both went into a confused and lengthy demand for the meaning of it all. Listening to them was painful and as they were making no sense at all there was no point in lingering.

"Santa Claus had better bring that pair a jug of room deodorizer for Christmas," Rhys observed.

"He'd better bring them a few brains if you ask me," Janet snapped. "Of all the pitiful ways to waste a person's time! If I ever thought Bert's boys would be dumb enough to do a thing like that, I'd . . . I don't know what I'd do."

"I doubt they will. Bert's kids have better things to do with their lives. Besides, pot costs money. It might not be the worst thing for Franny and Winny if Uncle Cyril did cut off their allowances and put them to work."

"Madoc, about that money your Aunt Oldrys left you. Is it really such an awful lot?"

"Not enough to turn our children into a pack of wasters, never fear. I'll have enough to buy my Jenny a nice little house with a nice big mortgage and leave some in the bank for a rainy day. Mostly we'll live on my weekly pay packet. Does that make you feel better?"

"Yes, if you want to know. Now that I've seen how the other half live, I'll be well pleased to settle for three square meals a day and a hired girl once a week till the babies get out of diapers."

"How many babies did you have in mind?"

"Oh, two or three, maybe."

"How about a set of triplets so we can get it over with all at once? On the other hand, I suppose it would be rather fun to see them coming along one after another."

"Not too soon after. We'll have to talk about that."

"We'll have to do more than talk, Jenny love."

"Oh, you!"

She poked him and blushed, so of course he had to respond in an appropriate manner. Herbert came along and caught them at it.

"My God, don't you two ever quit? We were just organizing a rescue party."

"Sorry." Madoc, somewhat red in the face, released Janet. "We ducked in through a side door. Now we're trying to find the shed where we park our snowshoes. I hope we haven't tracked up the floor too badly."

"Doesn't matter. It's just clean snow. Which door did you come in?"

"The one we happened to be close to is all I can tell you. We're hopelessly lost, I'm afraid. We've got mixed up in the hallways and haven't met a soul to set us straight till you came along." Just in case Herbert might think they'd discovered Franny and Winny. "Where is everyone?"

"Here and there. Babs and Clara are wrapping presents, I think. Val's washing her hair or some damn thing. Squire's playing bridge with Lawrence and Don and that poor chap Roy. Hell of a fix for Roy to be in. If he doesn't win with Don he'll get sacked, like as not. If he makes Squire lose, he won't get asked back. May's in the kitchen browbeating the cook and I was just on my way to check the stock. If it weren't for May and me, I can tell you, this place would fall to pieces pretty fast. I'd like to know what Cyril thinks he's . . ."

Herbert checked himself. "I assume you've noticed my brother-in-law has a drinking problem. Nice fellow, mind you, but he can do strange things when he's had one too many. But May can handle him. He's sleeping it off now, thank the Lord. Here, give me those snowshoes. I have to go out through the shed anyway. Go straight down the hall here till you come to a turn. Take a left, then a right. That will bring you out to the front staircase. I expect you can find your way from there, eh?"

They thanked him and did as he said, not meeting anyone else except Ludovic who relieved them of their wet jackets, expressed a polite hope they'd enjoyed their walk, and informed them that tea would be served at half past four in the back parlor.

"It will be a little early because of the mumming."

"And when are we expected to mum?" Rhys asked.

The butler permitted himself a smile. "At six o'clock or thereabout, sir. The waits will not be able to get here on account of the storm, but there will be music on the phonograph to play you in."

"We wait for the fanfare of trumpets, then come cavorting down the stairs, is that it?"

"That is approximately it, sir. I will inform Squire that you have returned safely."

"Please do," said Janet. "Explain that we didn't want to go tramping through the house in wet clothes and that we'll be happy to join him for tea later."

Ludovic received her message with a nod that was positively benign, and left to convey the joyful tidings. Janet and Madoc went on upstairs.

"Do you have all the doings for your mummery?" he asked her.

"Yes, Babs fixed me up after we'd finished the tree. I'm going to wash my own hair if Val's left any hot water, and do a little sewing."

"Do it in my room if you want to."

"Why? Aren't you going to be there?"

"Certainly. That's the whole point."

"Yes, well, I expect I'll get more done if I keep to my own."

"Cruel woman."

Rhys, reconciled to abandonment, closed his own door and stretched out to catch up on a little sleep, in case this turned out to be another busy night.

CHAPTER 11

Tea was a rather hit-or-miss affair, served more because this was part of the Graylings ritual than because people really wanted it, as far as Janet could see. Aunt Addie was the only one who paid much attention to the cake stand.

"I thought I'd make a good meal now because I may not get any dinner," she confided to Janet, who happened to be sitting beside her on the chesterfield.

"Oh, aren't you coming down for the mumming?" Janet asked.

"Yes, but I don't know how long I'll be staying. Rosa may want me, you see."

"I understand. It must be hard for you." Janet didn't know what else to say.

"No, I wouldn't call it hard. I'm expecting it, you see. Rosa and I always did stick together. Now you get on back upstairs and finish your pretty costume. I want to see you in it before I go."

Janet excused herself and did as she was bidden, much perturbed in mind. What on earth had Miss Adelaide been talking about? Was she beginning to wander a bit? Would it be a good idea to repeat that odd scrap of conversation to Babs or Squire or somebody?

The trouble was, they were all drifting away to get dressed for the mumming and by the time she'd made up her mind she ought to, there was nobody left to tell. Even Madoc was fussing that he'd slept longer than he'd meant to and must get bathed and changed, and did Jenny think he needed a shave?

She rubbed her cheek against his and decided he'd better because they hadn't tried out the kissing ball yet. In spite of everything, Janet couldn't help getting caught up in the excitement of dressing for a party. This would be something else to tell Annabelle, at any rate.

Val hadn't come down to tea. When Janet found her in the room they shared, she'd mellowed a fair amount, perhaps because she was having an attack of Yuletide spirit or perhaps because she needed to be zipped up the back. She'd arranged her blond hair in an updo with a topknot of pink silk roses and one long curl coming down over her right shoulder. Her costume was a court gown of pink brocade in the Watteau manner. Janet was able to tell her in all sincerity that she looked absolutely stunning.

"Like it? I had it made. Cost a fortune, but I knew Squire would be pleased enough with it to foot the bill. Now I'm just praying . . ."

A frown threatened to smudge her makeup and Val hastily smoothed out her face again. "Honestly, of all the times for Granny to die! You'd think she did it on purpose to spite us. Don't look so shocked. You don't know what an awful old crank she was. And now Uncle Cyril's all stirred up. I don't see why Squire couldn't have told us—oh, well, you're not interested in all this family stuff. I'd better see how Roy's getting on. Did you know his people are in oil?"

"Like sardines?" Janet couldn't resist saying.

Luckily Val was pleased enough with herself to be amused. "Pretty good. I'll have to tell Roy. Is Dafydd coming to your wedding?"

"I doubt it. He's going to do Wagner in Bayreuth, whatever that involves, then I believe he flies to San Francisco. Goodness knows if he'll ever make it back to New Brunswick."

"Dafydd's not much like his brother, is he?"

"No, I shouldn't say Dafydd was like Madoc," Janet replied in all sincerity. "You'd better do something about that top rose. It wobbles when you move."

Val concentrated again on her own toilette, then flew off to make sure Roy was resplendent enough to do her justice. Janet was free to arrange her own infinitely less ambitious effort. Without Val there to put her in the shade, she managed to convince herself she'd pass.

Madoc thought she would. "Jenny love, how beautiful you look. Where did you get that red blouse thing?"

"It's the top of my thermal underwear, but for goodness' sake don't tell anybody."

She'd basted tinsel rope around the neck and sleeves and added a long-tailed sash to camouflage the fact that the top was a different shade from the skirt. The tinsel crown hadn't worked out, so she'd swiped a spray of holly from the decorations on the zigzag staircase and wound it into a little coronet tied with red ribbon feloniously obtained from the same source.

"I don't quite know what I'm supposed to represent."

"You're my Christmas present, love. Hark, the herald angels sing."

An tinny blast from an old wind-up gramophone assailed their ears. Madoc picked up the plant stick that was to serve as his baton and offered Janet his arm.

"Shall we join the merrymakers, Lady Rhys? They've started the overture without the conductor. Won't do, you know. I shall take it up with the musicians' union."

Perhaps he wasn't supposed to be enjoying himself, but the way Janet filled out that transmogrified undervest roused visions of joys to come that might have brought disapproval from a Fundamentalist minister but felt pretty darned good to Detective Inspector Rhys.

"Oh, Madoc, wait." Janet made a little face. "There's something I ought to tell you. I hate to bring it up when we ought to be out there frisking, but I thought you'd better know."

She repeated what Aunt Addie had said at teatime. "I don't know whether she was feeling down in the mouth about Rosa or if she'd had another present'ment, or what. It almost sounds as if she might be thinking of suicide to me."

"Hard to say, love. When a person gets to be her age, whether or not to keep on living is mostly a matter of choice. It wouldn't be a bad idea for us to keep an eye on the old lady without being too conspicuous about it."

"Madoc, there is something going on, isn't there? Was Mrs. Condrycke murdered?"

He put his arms around her and laid his cheek against hers, prickly holly tickling his ear. "I'm inclined to think so, Jenny."

"And you haven't said so for fear of spoiling my fun. Madoc, you're not going to spend the rest of your life protecting the little woman?"

Somebody thumped on the door. "Come on, you two! Out of the hay and into the fray."

"Per order of May," added a voice that had to be Herbert's.

"We're ready. Sir Emlyn just had to find his baton." Madoc opened the door. "Now, ladies and shentlemen, if I am to contuct thiss choruss, I must remind you that it iss not enough to follow me. The itea iss to keep up with me, look you."

"We're two jumps ahead of you already."

Herbert and May were both dressed as lobsters, and acting as if they were already boiled. Their two sons were behind them, also wearing what Janet recognized with good reason as red thermal underwear. All four had huge red cardboard claws and feelers waving over their heads, and an assortment of extra legs and tails depending from their torsos.

"We're doing the Lobster Quadrille," shouted May. "Forward . . . crawl!"

The two boys were still giggling and acting silly. Their eyes were by now as red as their tails, Rhys noted. They must be new to marijuana, otherwise they'd be smart enough to have a bottle of patent eyewash on hand to take the redness out. Or else they were too stoned to give a hoot.

It was unlikely anyone but himself would notice. The oil lamps that Graylings depended on mostly for light didn't make much impression on these vast rooms. They were the perfect illumination for a masquerade, though. Costumes that might have looked tacky in daylight now took on an air of glamor and fantasy.

Val in her pink brocade and Roy in a white satin coat and knee breeches he'd no doubt rented from some theatrical costumer did make a striking couple. Donald was wearing knee breeches and cutaway coat like Roy's, though in a deep green well suited to his years and dignity. Babs had on a dress cut much like her daughter's, in emerald green with rose-colored ribbons. They made a most effective tableau grouped with their daughter and her escort.

Janet, who was aware of such things, couldn't help wondering if the parents had staged the whole scene for Roy's benefit. Maybe his people really were in oil, or maybe Babs and Donald found Val too much to handle and were hoping to see her safely tied down to a rising young junior executive who seemed only too willing to embrace the Condrycke lifestyle. There was no denying a white wig with a black ribbon at the back did something for a man. Even May was giving Roy what might be described as an interested eye, and Val had quite forgotten to look petulant.

Clara was a flapper, complete with cloche hat and rolled stockings with Christmas seals stuck on her knees. Lawrence had blossomed forth in a raccoon coat, a porkpie hat, and a fake red poinsettia as a boutonnière.

Aunt Addie looked vaguely Elizabethan in a black velvet gown with so much fullness in the skirt it must date from the age of hoops and petticoats. She had real lace over her hair and shoulders, and a parure of jet and garnet brooches, bracelets, finger rings, earrings, an ornate necklace, and an involved arrangement of chains and pendants that Rhys thought he'd heard referred to as a lavaliere. If the old lady was indeed contemplating her own departure from the scene, she clearly intended to go out in style.

Miss Adelaide was on the arm of Squire Condrycke, and a magnificent sight was he. His costume must be one he wore every year, for surely nobody would go to that much trouble and expense for a one-time performance. The only word for it was regal. He looked like Henry the Eighth on his way to marry some wife or other—probably Anne of Cleves, considering the family penchant for big blonds. Over a doublet and hose of richest purple velvet slashed with red satin he wore a long crimson velvet cape edged in what looked like ermine, though it was more likely white rabbit. A floppy cap of the same crimson velvet edged with the same white fur needed only a circlet of gold to turn it into a crown.

Janet won favor by dropping him a low curtsy. Then she heard a shout from down the hall.

"Don't I get one, too?"

It was Cyril, got up in what was plainly meant to be a merciless parody of his father's elegance. He'd put on a suit of ordinary long underwear and over it a pair of what Janet guessed had once been May's gym bloomers. His royal cape was a blanket fastened with a big safety pin and his headgear a paper cap edged with cotton batting. Even as she made a second curtsy to keep the peace, Janet couldn't help wondering why nobody had yet kicked him downstairs.

The Condryckes must be a remarkably forbearing lot. They seemed, no doubt wisely, to have accepted Cyril in the role of Merry-Andrew and let him lead their dance, or whatever it was supposed to be. They were all bouncing along with a sort of skipping step that was rather fun to do. Since the ancient gramophone was so limited in its scope, Babs had ingeniously taped a number of lively jigs, carols, folk tunes, morris dances, and similar sounds of the Merrie England Squire thought he was reproducing here, and carried the little bat-

tery-operated tape recorder more or less concealed by a berib-
boned green satin muff to give them music along their way.

Madoc Rhys wondered if they planned to do a Sir Roger de
Coverley or anything of that sort, and meanly hoped they
would because he'd learned the steps at his great-uncle's and
Roy almost certainly didn't know them. There was something
about a chap who stood six foot two in his white satin pumps
with the bows on the toes that couldn't help making a man
who barely made five foot eight in his brother's old dinner
jacket feel insignificant. Still, there was the fact that Roy had
wound up stuck with Val while he himself had Janet.

Cyril was cock-a-hoop enough for an army. He leaped and
cavorted, did alarming things on that treacherous staircase.
At one point he performed a back somersault over the banister
but managed to keep his grip on the railing and flip himself
back again. Somebody must surely have been thinking, "Too
bad."

They jigged on through the Great Hall, pausing to bow to
the Christmas tree and to accept some other no doubt tradi-
tional and assuredly potent libation from Ludovic. Thus stim-
ulated they continued their Bacchanalian dance, twisting
through corridors as crazily laid out as the staircase, catching
glimpses of rooms Janet yearned to have a proper look at. If
this was the guided tour she'd been promised, she didn't think
much of it. Furthermore, she was beginning to feel winded.

At least the exercise kept one warm, not to mention the ad-
ditional potations along the way. There was another ritual
drink with the cook, in a vast, stone-flagged kitchen where
Janet would have loved to linger and admire. This was the
first she and Madoc had seen of the staff. There were a couple
of maids in real gray uniforms with real white aprons, and
some men who must be the Sam Neddicks of the estab-
lishment.

Squire began to deliver a kindly condescending set speech
in French. Cyril wouldn't let him go on.

"Knock it off, Squire. They've heard it all before and they don't believe it anyway," which might have been true but could not have been ruder.

The rest of the Condryckes tried awfully hard to pretend this was all part of the fun, but the staff, who no doubt understood English perfectly well, looked sour.

"I shouldn't be surprised if Cyril just won a few votes for the Quebec Libre faction," Madoc murmured to Janet.

He and she had dropped to the rear of the procession and weren't making more than the odd token effort to keep up with the hopping and skipping. Cyril stayed in the lead, cutting such outrageous capers that Rhys began to wonder if he was merely drunk or something more. Eventually the procession wound its way back to the Great Hall, where Ludovic was waiting to announce dinner. Roast suckling pig tonight, Squire had said. Rhys couldn't say he was looking forward to it.

There was one big advantage in going to the table. Cyril seated with a full glass of wine in front of him was less obnoxious than Cyril in motion. He did clamor for Janet to sit beside him, but Rhys was having none of that.

"Janet has a previous engagement," he said with a gentle but meaningful smile.

The Condryckes obliged him by the usual uproar of laughter, but Rhys could see wary looks exchanged, especially between May and Herbert. Cyril was making a real play for the lovely young stranger. He wasn't going to get Janet, but his new-found opulence might lead him to think of buying himself a bride, and brides were apt to have babies.

Franny or Winny, whichever was the elder, must be in line to inherit Graylings some day. Donald would get it first, of course, assuming he outlived Cyril, but Donald had only a daughter. Maybe that was why he and Babs were countenancing Val's romance with big, blond Roy who looked as if he could beget big, blond sons in the true Condrycke tradition.

Clara's nonpresent son must be older than May's boys but even he, being far away and not interested enough to come home for the holidays, would be a far better bet as heir than a woman who'd want to move in and take over Graylings without regard for the family. And Donald would surely be an obliging heir apparent.

Rhys thought he had Donald tabbed by now. He was indeed the sort who'd smile at the kid who ran the elevator. He'd be pleasant to everybody, because being pleasant was probably what Donald was best at. No doubt he held his position on the company board because the Condryckes were major stockholders and Donald was not a man to ask awkward questions or cast a dissenting vote at the wrong time.

Janet said she hadn't seen him around the office much, probably because he was seldom there. He must serve on other boards where a distinguished name and an agreeable manner would be welcomed and his own company's prestige thereby enhanced. He'd appear in the right places, make the witty little speeches bright young men like Roy wrote for him, and do a pretty good public relations job, all in all.

If Babs enjoyed the social whirl, as she gave every appearance of doing, she and Donald must lead an agreeable life together. They must value Graylings as a place to invite important people who'd like a weekend of hunting or fishing or boating or sitting at the bridge table with Ludovic bringing them drinks and Squire being gallant. Inviting amusing people like younger sons of famous conductors would add to the Graylings charisma. Rhys wondered at how many houseparties his and Jenny's names would get dropped during the next six months.

May and Clara, as well as Squire who clearly loved to shine, must depend on Donald and Babs to supply them with diverting company. There appeared to be so much warmth among the Condryckes and their spouses that guests would be charmed, as a rule. Last night, one would have thought Cyril was as well disposed as the rest of them; but that couldn't be so or the man wouldn't be doing all this spiteful crowing now regardless of what he'd got inside him.

Perhaps if one probed deeper, the other relationships weren't any too harmonious, either. Those practical jokes they were so fond of springing on each other didn't arise from the same kind of mutual respect and affection that existed at the Wadmans'. He couldn't see Bert dropping a plastic lizard down Janet's or Annabelle's back, though he could easily see Bert getting crowned with a frying pan if he tried. Yet either of them would give Bert her last pint of blood if he really needed it.

Aunt Addie must have decided Rosa could spare her. She'd stayed on to dinner and didn't seem to be suffering any lack of appetite. It was hard to believe a woman who could eat that much roast pork at night was in immediate danger of shuffling off her mortal coil, unless perhaps from acute indigestion. Rhys made a mental note never to have roast suckling pig served at his own festive board.

His Jenny was of the same mind. Having grown up on a farm, she knew animals were raised to be eaten and she wasn't squeamish as a rule, but she did murmur to Madoc, "I can't help feeling sorry for the poor little thing," and left most of her helping for Ludovic to take away.

May noticed. "Don't you like it, Janet?" she bellowed in a hurt tone.

"It's just that I made such a pig of myself at tea I feel guilty eating one of my own kind," she replied.

That got a great laugh. The Condryckes were really straining for mirth tonight. Squire was less chatty than usual, no doubt because Cyril was picking up everything he said and either contradicting or mocking him in a way that penetrated even the scarlet carapaces of May and Herbert. He was eating next to nothing but drinking everything within his reach; even water, although that was most likely by accident.

As on the previous evening, there was too much food and the meal lasted far too long. Dessert was mince pie, which both Madoc and Janet liked but could by then have done without. After that came a complicated savory made with little grilled fishes out of the bay. Fifine caught them in summertime on her hours off and salted them down in crocks for the winter, according to Clara. Janet, used to finishing her meal with the sweet and another cup of tea in the comfortable farm fashion, thought it sounded like a lot of bother for little result. She hoped Madoc wouldn't expect his wife to fuss with this kind of culinary frippery.

May suggested coffee in the library again, but Cyril turned cantankerous. He was really drunk by now, but unfortunately not quite drunk enough. That nap after lunch and the wild careering through the house must have perked him up. He wanted coffee in the Great Hall with the Yule log blazing and everybody singing "Rudolph the Red-Nosed Reindeer" in the jolly old Merrie English tradition.

This was another poke at Squire, but everyone pretended to think he was being funny. Val, who'd decided which side her bread was buttered on, loudly seconded darling Unkie and the motion was carried.

CHAPTER 12

"Line up, everybody. Now, ah-one, ah-two . . ."

Cyril was braying like, as Bert Wadman would say, a jack-ass, conducting his none too willing chorus with a baton that would have been more suited to a pipe band. The stick was at least three feet long and had a heavy, ornate silver knob at one end and a silver ferrule at the other.

Janet, who'd maneuvered herself next to Miss Adelaide, heard the old woman catch her breath as the silver knob caught a glint from the battery lantern behind the Christmas tree.

"That's Rosa's cane he's got. He must have gone into her room and taken it. I left it right beside her bed where she always kept it. Cyril, you mustn't do that! It's mocking the dead."

"And what's the dead going to do about it?" he mocked back. "You'd better be damned careful with that tongue of yours from here on in, Auntie dear. It's my charity you've been living on all these years while Squire's been playing Lord of the Manor, dealing out the dollars as if they belonged to him instead of me. No wonder he could afford to be so cursed generous. You and your Goddamned Christmas spirit!"

Cyril turned on his father, brandishing the cane as though to strike him down. Squire didn't flinch.

"Cyril, as we've been trying to tell you all day, you do not understand the situation. You are in fact the titular owner of Graylings, but as long as I am alive and capable, I hold full administrative . . ."

"Hark!"

If Aunt Addie was doing it for effect, she couldn't have chosen a more dramatic moment. Even Cyril froze with the cane in midair.

"It's coming again. I can hear it."

With one accord they broke formation and raced for the windows. Sure enough, there was the eerie glow, the blazing spires flickering against the uncertain background of the falling snow, so close tonight that it seemed they could almost reach out and touch the Phantom Ship of Bay Chaleur.

Val screamed. So did Clara. Aunt Addie, predictably, fainted. Madoc Rhys took one startled glance, then whispered to Janet, "Stay here with the others," and melted backward out of the room.

Nobody but herself saw him go. They were all watching the ship as though they'd never seen it before.

"It's never been twice in a row like this," Squire muttered. "Never in all the years I've lived here."

"It's coming for you, Squire!" Cyril was hilarious. Surely it couldn't have been only the liquor that was making him act so wild. "Go on out. I'll open the door."

"Cyril, don't!"

Aunt Addie had revived, more quickly than the last time. "Don't make a mockery. You're tempting fate."

Donald helped the old woman to her feet. She smoothed down her bunchy black velvet skirt and straightened her lace. "I'm going up to Rosa. You'd better let me take that cane, or she may come looking for it herself."

Now what to do? Janet stood hesitating. Madoc had said they'd better look after Aunt Addie, but he'd also told her to stay here with the rest of the Condryckes. Which should she do? She took a tentative step toward the doorway, Cyril noticed and sprang to plant himself under the kissing ball, waving Granny's silver-mounted cane like a great, beckoning finger.

"Right this way, Janet. I'm puckered and waiting."

That settled it. She couldn't leave the room without passing under the mistletoe, and not for anything in this world would she let herself be pawed by that leering, mouthing, flailing creature. Janet pretended she hadn't heard and moved closer to the fire as if to warm away the chill the ship had brought to Graylings. Old Adelaide, though, walked right up and shook her head at her great-nephew.

"Cyril, you've got to stop this or something dreadful's going to happen. Janet's not for you. I told you that before. You've had your fair share and you're not getting any more. Now come along to bed like a good boy or you'll wake up to an empty Christmas stocking."

Incredibly, Cyril turned to follow her. Squire looked at May.

"Don't look at me," she told him. "He's your son. Sorry, Squire, but I've had all I can take of Cyril for one day. Come on, everybody, pull up your chairs to the fire and let's get thawed out. Clara, Lawrence. Boys, do something about a chair for your poor old Mum. Come on back here, Babs. Aunt Addie can take care of herself."

"I'm not going after her. I need to powder my nose, as we used to say before it was considered acceptable to mention bathrooms in society. Pour me a brandy and save me a place."

There was a good deal of milling around for a while. Janet tried to keep track of who was where, but with the flickering firelight, the dim oil lamps with their chimneys sooted up from the drafts caused when the window curtains were drawn on account of the Phantom Ship's second appearance, and the fact that the batteries in the lantern that had been illuminating the Christmas tree chose this inopportune time to run down, she had to give it up as a bad job. All she could do was find herself a place near the fire, make sure there was room beside her for Madoc, and wish to goodness he'd come back. She let Ludovic talk her into a tiny glass of Cointreau and was sipping at it when she heard Babs screaming from the hallway.

"Cyril, no! Have you lost your mind completely? She'll freeze to death out there. Get away from that door! Oh, God, help! Quick, somebody, help me!"

"Good God!"

Donald was on his feet, running. Herbert, Lawrence, the whole flock of them charged after him. Janet got caught up in their midst, wedged in between Val who kept tripping over her long skirts and Squire, whose age and girth didn't make for speed. She could hear Babs still screaming, pleading, struggling. Cyril was making noises like an animal. He must have gone totally berserk.

"She's out there," Babs panted when they got to her. "I can't make him open the door."

Cyril had his back to the thick oaken planks, still flailing away with Granny's cane. Babs had a welt on her cheek. The elegant gown was half off her shoulders, her wig on the floor, her hair a mess. Donald and the other men waded in regardless of the heavy stick, wrestled it away from Cyril, hurled him away from the door, and wrenched it open.

"My God! You can't see your hand in front of you," gasped Lawrence.

"Get some lamps," ordered Squire, back in charge now. "Hold my hand, Herbert. David, Lawrence, make a human chain. For God's sake don't let go. She must be right here somewhere. Val, open the curtains. Give us any light there is."

There was something majestic in the old man as he wrapped the rabbit-trimmed velvet mantle around him and stepped forward into the slashing whiteness. The blast that came through the open door was straight from the North Pole, but nobody seemed to feel it. Clara and May were tending to Babs, who was in hysterics by now. Janet stood there holding a lamp, praying it wouldn't blow out. They were all screaming, "Aunt Addie! Aunt Addie!"

Madoc rushed in from wherever he'd been, snatched the lamp, and thrust Janet out of the worst of the draft. It was probably not more than a minute but it seemed like eternity before the light picked up a black lump in the snow and Squire bent to scoop up the old woman.

"Change hands with me, Squire. You can't carry her. For God's sake hang on to me, Herb," shouted Donald.

He picked up the old woman, her arms hanging stiff and her head lolling down, and the human chain dragged them inside the house.

"Get her to the fire, quick! Val, run up and fetch some blankets. Clara, bring some hot towels, hot-water bottles, any damned hot thing you can lay your hands on. Hurry."

May was in charge now, hustling them back into the Great Hall, shoving a chesterfield so close to the fireplace it seemed the upholstery must go up in flames, laying Aunt Addie down on it, chafing her hands, ordering somebody to pull off her snow-filled shoes, her frozen skirt; screaming at Donald to put his coat around Babs and give her some brandy before she caught her death.

"For God's sake where's Val with those blankets? Auntie will get pneumonia."

"I don't think so." Madoc Rhys was standing behind the sofa, his arms tight around Janet. "I think she's past it."

Nobody paid any attention to him except Janet herself. She twisted around to face him.

"Madoc, I didn't know what to do. She went out and I started to follow her, but Cyril got under the kissing ball and was yelling at me to come over and . . ."

"Sh-h, darling. It's all right. Thank God you didn't wind up out there with her."

Babs was standing as close to the fire as she could get, sipping from a glass of brandy Donald was holding for her, huddling his dark green brocade coat around her ruined finery.

"He just seemed to go crazy. I don't know what happened. When I realized she was out there he—I tried to make him open the door and he kept hitting at me with that cane. I thought he was going to poke my eyes out. I couldn't—this stupid arm of mine—I'm afraid I've put up a bad show."

"Don't be silly, Mother, you probably saved her life."

Val had come back with the blankets and was wrapping one around her mother, who couldn't stop shivering. "Daddy, I think Mama's in shock. Can't we get her up to bed?"

"No, I'm all right. Truly, darling," Babs protested. "I have to see if Aunt Addie's—where's Cyril?"

"He was out in the hall when I came through. Roy's holding him and Uncle Lawrence is trying to get some sense out of him. He can't even seem to recall what he did."

"Herbert, go help them," snapped Squire. "Get him up to his room and lock him in till he comes to his senses."

"Franny and Winny can go," said May. "I want Herb with me."

Clara brought hot-water bottles. May reached under the blankets and stripped off Aunt Addie's undergarments, now wet from thawing snow. They rubbed, they slapped, they tried against all tenets of sound first-aid practice to get her to swallow some brandy. The liquid ran out the side of her half-open mouth.

"She's not getting warm," Clara said in a puzzled voice. "Why isn't she getting warm?"

"Keep at it," panted May. "Put some more logs on the fire, can't you, Herb?"

"It's hot enough to roast an ox already."

Herbert was sweating, wiping his head with the back of his sleeve. One of his cardboard lobster claws was broken and flapping absurdly down over his eyes, the other wilted and curving backward. May looked like a pictorial nightmare by Hieronymus Bosch. The whole scene was a fantasy: the limp, unresponding figure on the opulent sofa with the leaping fire behind, the wet clothes dropped on the floor, the anxious faces above the frivolous costumes.

And still Aunt Addie did not respond. Squire tried to put

through a call to a doctor in Dalhousie for advice, but the line was dead. Babs thought of taking the old woman's temperature and found it under ninety degrees. When May tried again a little later it was two degrees lower. Madoc Rhys suggested holding a mirror to Miss Adelaide's mouth. It remained unclouded. There was no pulse, no heartbeat. Still May wouldn't give up.

"I've read about people being underwater for half an hour and still coming round. If they're cold enough . . ."

"God knows she's cold enough!" Clara was getting hysterical.

"I'm afraid," said Madoc Rhys, "that people who've been revived after long immersion were given special treatment in hospitals. Fluids were administered intravenously and other things done that we couldn't manage here. There is also the problem of not all the body organs beginning to work at once even if resuscitation begins. If the head warms up before the heart, for instance, brain cells may be killed. Toxicity may destroy the liver before it can begin excreting. Also, I believe the lowest body temperature at which anybody has so far been known to survive is eighty-eight."

"I don't care," said May. "She's getting warmer. I can feel it."

"That's the hot-water bottles," Clara argued. "Oh, God, my arms are ready to drop off. Take her temperature again, Babs."

It was eighty-five. May wouldn't let them stop until an hour had passed and the thermometer registered eighty degrees Fahrenheit. At that she sat down and buried her face in her hands, the red cardboard lobster claws still waving grotesquely over her bent head.

"She's gone."

"And Cyril's a murderer."

CHAPTER 13

That was Lawrence, tying up the loose ends in his precise, legal way. May flew at him.

"Did you have to say that? Where is he? What have you done with him?"

"Exactly what Squire told us to, took him up to his room and locked him in. He was out on his feet before we'd even got him upstairs. Here's the key, Squire. You'd better keep it. I don't want the responsibility."

"I do, if you don't mind."

Madoc Rhys stepped between Squire and Lawrence, his hand outstretched.

"You? What the hell for? It's none of your business."

"But it is, you see."

Rhys pulled out his wallet and showed his credentials. Lawrence, agape, read them off.

"Detective Inspector Madoc Rhys, Royal Canadian Mounted Police. What the hell? You said you worked for the government."

"I do."

"In research," Donald added numbly.

"My mother said that. She is embarrassed by my profession. I did not contradict her because it is quite true that I do research. Right now I shall have to start researching the murder of your aunt because that is my job, you see."

"My God, a Mountie!"

Herbert found that funny, for some reason. Maybe he was drunk or hysterical or a little of both. Maybe he just needed a laugh.

"Now," said Rhys, "it is the usual procedure for me to take statements from you all. A matter of form, you understand. Janet, is your shorthand up to taking notes?"

"I can make a stab at it, anyway."

"Then, if I could trouble you for paper and a pen, Ludovic?"

"But surely," Squire stepped forward, his crimson mantle wrapped around him like a toga, "as Sir Emlyn's son . . . you couldn't . . . a breach of hospitality . . ."

"You and my mother would be in full agreement on that point, Squire Condrycke," Madoc Rhys replied. "It is a social outrage for me to be doing these things. However, it would be a dereliction of duty for me not to do them. Then I should be fired and what would become of my wife? Also, I must point out to you that it is going to look very strange when that undertaker shows up and finds two bodies instead of one. It will be less awkward for you all, believe me, that this dreadful occurrence should be handled in a proper and official manner. Lawrence will appreciate the force of my argument. Also, being your legal adviser, he can counsel you as to your rights and duties with regard to answering my questions."

"The man's right," said Lawrence. "Do it and get it over with. We've nothing to hide. Babs, you saw Cyril shove her out."

"No, I didn't. Anyway, it was only a . . . a prank. I'm sure he didn't mean to."

"Babs, if he meant it as a prank then it would be impossible for him not to mean it at all," said Rhys. "Could you be more explicit, please?"

She shook her head. "I don't know. I'm so bewildered. I suppose what I meant was that Cyril didn't mean to kill Aunt Addie. He'd been drinking a lot, as I'm sure I don't have to tell you. When the Phantom Ship appeared the second night in a row and she went into her usual performance . . . I'm sorry, that sounds unkind. Anyway, she'd been getting at him about fooling around with Granny's cane and mocking the dead. You heard her. He—I don't know what got into him. Cyril hasn't been himself all day. Has he, May? Have you ever seen him carry on the way he did tonight?"

"Excuse me," said Rhys. "I am the one who's supposed to be asking the questions just now. Your sister-in-law will have her turn. Could you simply describe to me the actual physical acts that took place, without regard to what anybody may have been thinking at the time?"

"Where do you want me to start?"

"What prompted you to leave the Great Hall?"

"I had to go to the bathroom, since you're interested in physical acts. Didn't you hear me say so?"

Rhys merely continued his questioning.

"Where were Cyril and his aunt when you made this decision?"

"In the front hall, I suppose."

"Why do you suppose so?"

"Because they'd left the Great Hall just before me, naturally." Babs was sounding irritated. "You must remember. Cyril had been standing under the kissing ball trying to coax Janet over to him. If she'd been a bit less prissy about it—but I'm not supposed to engage in conjecture, am I?"

So now it was Janet's fault for refusing to be mauled by Cyril and getting him into a temper. No doubt the Condryckes would cling to that belief, especially since Sir Emlyn's son had turned out a traitor to his alleged class. Two worms in the same bud.

"You don't have to write all that down, Jenny love. Just the part about their leaving the room. Did they go together or separately?"

"Together, of course," said Babs. "Aunt Addie told him to come along with her and for a wonder, he went. Why do we have to go over all this stuff? You were here, weren't you?"

The answer was no, but Rhys was not about to give it. "I am following customary police procedure," he explained. "This is the pettifogging way we have to operate. Lawrence will tell you how important it is to conform to the letter of the law."

"Answer him, Babs," Lawrence obliged by saying. "You have nothing to be afraid of. Rhys is right. The more open we are, the less scandal there'll be. Even Rhys himself can testify to the fact that Cyril was behaving in a totally irrational way. I'm sure we can get him off on a plea of . . . well, I shall have to take advice before I commit myself. I'm not a criminal lawyer, you know, despite local gossip to the contrary. Cyril will wind up spending some time in a sanatorium, I expect, which will do him no harm. Tell the truth and shame the devil."

The devil in this case being Rhys, from the glares he was getting. Babs went on with her tale.

"My assumption that Cyril and Aunt Addie were in the front hall when I told May I was going to the bathroom is based on the fact that they went out before me and were still there when I passed them. I was in a hurry, to be as blunt as possible."

"What were they doing when you passed them?"

"I couldn't say. My impression is that they were standing there talking, but they may have been walking. Auntie moved very slowly sometimes, and she'd have been tired from the mumming and the dinner. But that's conjecture, isn't it? I just don't know. I didn't look back. I went directly up the stairs— that is, as directly as possible—and along the hallway to the bathroom, where I used the facilities in the customary manner."

May emitted a nervous snicker. Rhys asked, "Was anybody else upstairs at the time?"

"I couldn't say. You know how the bathrooms are arranged, all together. The first one happened to be vacant, so I used it. I had no reason to go poking into the others, so I didn't."

"You didn't return to your bedroom to fix your hair or whatever?"

"I was wearing a wig," Babs reminded him. "I would have

had no occasion to fix my hair. I washed my hands, touched up my lipstick in the bathroom mirror, and came straight back down. Altogether I don't suppose I was up there more than two or three minutes. It was cold in the hallways and I wanted to get back to the fire."

"Would you say it was unusually cold?"

"I thought so. I put it down to the fact that I was wearing a costume instead of the warmer clothes I'd normally have on. It didn't occur to me that Cyril might have opened the door, even though he was standing in front of it when I next saw him."

"When did you see him?"

"As I was coming down the stairs. I didn't see Aunt Addie but you know how the staircase twists and turns, and the light isn't much good in the hall. When I got close enough to see that he was alone, I said, 'Where's Aunt Addie? I thought you two were going up together,' or something of the sort. I daresay I sounded as annoyed as I felt. I'd hoped we were rid of Cyril for the evening. I'm sorry, Squire, but . . ."

"That's quite all right, Babs," said her father-in-law. "So had we all. What did Cyril tell you?"

"At first he just leaned against the door and smiled that same silly grin he'd had plastered to his face all evening, so I asked him again. By then I was beginning to feel worried, though I didn't quite know why. Because of Granny, I suppose. Anyway, I think I said, 'Did she go upstairs?' and he answered, 'No, she went to see the Phantom Ship.'

"Even then it didn't register. I thought he meant she'd gone into the small parlor on the other side of the foyer to see if she could get a last glimpse of the ship from the bay window that faces west. I stuck my head in there and called, 'Aunt Addie?' But she wasn't there. Then it dawned on me what he might have meant, and I ran back to the door. Cyril was still there with that same silly grin on his face. I said, 'Cyril, she's not outside?' and he said again, 'She went to see the Phantom Ship.'

"That was when I panicked. I tried to open the door and he wouldn't let me near it. I struggled with him and he started hitting me with Granny's cane and I was screaming . . ."

Babs began to tremble again. Donald put his arm around her.

"Now, Babs, try to calm yourself. We all know you did everything you could. Rhys, if you're through badgering my wife, I'd like to take her upstairs. It hasn't escaped your investigative mind, I trust, that she's sustained physical injury as well as severe psychological shock?"

"It has not escaped me. I have finished with her and you may certainly take her upstairs as soon as I have finished with you."

"With me? What can I say? I was simply here with everyone else. Helping May arrange chairs around the fireplace, as I recall."

"Did you see your brother under the kissing ball?"

"Of course I did. He was waving that damned cane and yelling to Janet to come and kiss him, or words to that effect."

"And did you see what Janet did?"

"She turned her back on him in a rather prim and ladylike fashion and went over to the fireplace. My sister May had been trying to get us to sit down. No, wait, that was after Cyril left the room that we sat down. Anyway, Aunt Addie went over and spoke to Cyril after he'd called out to Janet and said something I didn't catch. The pair of them left the room, much to my personal relief, and that was when May said something to the effect of let's all sit down and be comfortable. Since Janet was already by the fireplace, I got a chair for her, which she took. We were all finding seats and getting settled when my wife began screaming from the front hall."

"Do you corroborate that, Janet?" asked Rhys.

"Yes, that's right," she answered. "I didn't want to make a scene by refusing point-blank, so I made believe I didn't hear

Cyril and was just going to warm myself. I probably did look prim. You're always saying I do. Anyway, Donald did bring me a chair and I sat down and Ludovic brought me a liqueur. I didn't see Aunt Addie and Cyril go out because I had to pretend I wasn't noticing him, but when I did look at the doorway again they were both gone. Aunt Addie had said she was going up to Rosa so I assumed she had. People were milling around, as Donald says. I honestly couldn't tell you who was in the room and who wasn't, but I do remember his giving me the chair and then being the first one to run out when Babs started calling for help."

"Thank you, Janet," said Donald. "Rhys, do I gather I now have an alibi for the crime my brother committed? If in fact it can be counted as a crime."

"I am only trying to establish the facts beyond any possibility of doubt," Rhys repeated in his patient, gentle voice. "Did you hear your aunt talking to your brother?"

"What difference does it make?"

"It could make a difference if your aunt had said something of a nature so inflammatory as to arouse your brother's anger against her."

"Oh, I see what you're driving at. I do beg your pardon, Rhys. This is the first time I've ever been involved in anything of this sort, needless to say. I'm rattled and I've been rude. Aunt Addie did get at Cyril a bit about using Granny's cane. She'd say anything that came into her head, especially when one of her oracular fits was upon her. I can't recall anything particularly inflammatory. Of course I wasn't close enough to hear what she said when they were over by the doorway. Perhaps someone else heard? Sorry, it's your province to ask the questions, isn't it."

"Yes, but I shall be glad if anyone has an answer."

Clara was prepared. "I heard her. She told Cyril he had to stop what he was doing or something dreadful would happen. She said Janet wasn't for him and she'd told him that before. She said he'd got his fair share and he wouldn't get any more.

I don't know what she meant by that, but it's what she said. Then she told him he wouldn't get anything in his Christmas stocking if he didn't behave himself and go to bed. It sounds ridiculous, but that's what she said. And then he turned around and went out with her."

"Do you mean beside, behind, or in front of her?"

"Behind, I think. I couldn't say for sure. Aunt Addie had on that black gown and it was dark over by the doorway, as Babs said. Still is, for that matter, as you can see for yourself. You can barely see the kissing ball from here. I don't see why your prissy little Janet had to make such a fuss about nothing. If anybody antagonized Cyril, she was the one. What's such a big deal about giving someone a kiss under the mistletoe at Christmastime, will you kindly tell me that?"

"Refusing a man a kiss does not as a rule constitute incitement to murder, especially when the man is so casual an acquaintance as your brother Cyril," Rhys answered gravely. "We shall, however, let it stand in the record that Janet Wadman did in fact refrain from crossing a large room to kiss a drunken man who was brandishing a somewhat formidable weapon with which he is alleged to have subsequently belabored his own sister-in-law after having thrust his aged great-aunt out into a snow squall at twenty-eight degrees below zero Fahrenheit. Please make careful note of your recreant behavior, Janet."

"Sure, go ahead and cover up for her," cried Val, "but what did Aunt Addie mean when she told Cyril he'd got his share and wasn't going to get any more?"

"It certainly didn't mean he'd got his share of me, if that's what you're driving at," Janet retorted. "I don't go in for fun and games, as you have reason to know."

"Why does my daughter have reason to know a thing like that?" Donald asked with ice in his voice.

Janet flushed as red as her costume. It wasn't fair to get Val in trouble for trying to stand up for her own flesh and blood.

"Because Val and I are sharing a room, of course. She's been with me whenever I might otherwise have been doing what she knows darn well I wasn't."

"Fair enough. Put that in the record, too, eh, Madoc?" said Herbert. "Say, is it against the rules for us to have a swig of that brandy we were supposed to be getting after dinner? And for God's sake can't we take poor old Aunt Addie out of here? It gives me the willies, seeing her stretched out like that."

"In just a moment."

Aunt Addie's presence couldn't be all that harrowing, since nothing was visible but a roll of blankets on the couch. Rhys went on taking statements, for what they were worth.

The British lady with the facile pen would have her suspects herded into one room where a wily minion from the constabulary was covertly watching their behavior and then ushering them one by one into the inner sanctum where her hero would ask each separate suspect the craftiest possible questions and get the fraughtest answers imaginable. The Mountie hadn't a minion to his name unless he counted Janet, and he was not about to let her loose again among this lot.

Everybody agreed that there'd been a certain amount of confusion what with the Phantom Ship's arrival, Cyril's theatrics, and May's attempt to get them all comfortable again before Babs started screaming in the hall. They were all quite sure they could vouch for each other, but as nobody happened to have noticed Rhys himself hadn't been among them, he had to take the group alibi for what it was worth.

He went doggedly down the list, however, extracting whatever he could from each one in turn. At last he said, "And now one last question, after which you are all free to do as you please. Can anyone tell me what kind of amphetamines Cyril has been taking?"

CHAPTER 14

"Amphetamines?"

That stirred them up.

"You mean speed?" said Winny, most injudiciously.

"What the hell do you know about speed?" yelped Herbert. "You and Franny haven't been monkeying around with that stuff, for Christ's sake?"

"They give us lectures about drugs at school," Franny assured his father. "Shut up, Win. Don't go trying to show off."

"Amphetamines can be found in certain prescribed medications, such as diet pills," Rhys explained. "Cyril may have been taking them on a doctor's orders."

Clara shook her head. "Cyril hasn't gone near a doctor in years. He's afraid he might get shipped off somewhere to dry out."

"Is anybody else among you taking any such medication?"

"Of course not," said May. "Why should we?"

"We're all healthy as horses," Herbert added.

"What about your employees?"

"They wouldn't spend the money. Anyway, they know damn well they'd get fired if they got up to anything funny around here," the steward insisted. "Squire runs a tight ship."

"Well, however he got it, Cyril Condrycke showed every sign this evening of being under the influence of amphetamines," Rhys insisted. "His aggressive actions and his bizarre, hyperactive antics during that march he led us earlier, which I gather you all found uncharacteristic of Cyril, were in sharp contrast to the manner he evinced last evening. Have you ever observed such marked swings in his behavior before?

Clara, you see a fair amount of Cyril, don't you? What is your opinion?"

He asked Clara because he thought her the least apt to be overcharitable, and Clara did not let him down.

"I've never in my life seen Cyril act like that before. Usually he comes down with a bad back if you so much as ask him to hand you a sofa cushion. I don't say he's not an awful tease, because he can drive you straight to distraction without half trying. He used to get Granny steamed up about something, for instance, then clear out and leave the rest of us to bear the brunt of her temper. He never does anything but talk, though. I've been wondering all day why he's acted so strangely. Nobody was going to convince me he's tearing himself to pieces over dear old Granny any more than the rest of us are. I assumed it must have had something to do with that meeting this morning, but Lawrence says Cyril didn't hear anything then that he hadn't known before."

"My wife is right, Inspector, if that's what we ought to be calling you now," Lawrence corroborated. "Cyril may not fully understand his position now and he obviously didn't before, but that's not because it has never been explained to him. Cyril always knew he was the titular heir to Graylings. His grandfather had delusions of grandeur, not to put too fine a point on it, and he thought it would be a grand idea to start a family entail like all the dukes and earls back home."

The lawyer sniffed to show what he thought of dukes and earls. "Luckily, the old man was very much under his wife's thumb. Granny may not have had the world's sweetest disposition, but she always did have a sound head on her shoulders and thank God she did. It was she who dictated the terms of her husband's will. She conceded that Cyril was to inherit the property, but she also stipulated that she herself was to retain control of it for as long as she lived, with Squire as her managing agent, if you want to use that term."

"Squire was already functioning in that capacity?" Rhys asked.

"Oh, yes. Had been for some time, and doing a damned good job if it, by and large. Squire's position had in fact already been assured to him when he consented to take the Condrycke name at the time of his marriage to the Condryckes' daughter, an only child. I'm telling you this because it's a matter of public record and because we've nothing to hide. Squire has acted in strict accordance with his father-in-law's will and with his own wife's dying wish that all their children should be given equal opportunity to share in the benefits from the estate according to their needs and, within reason, their wishes, unless they proved totally undeserving. The Graylings property is a large one, and as all have contributed in one way or another toward keeping it going, all have duly benefited. Cyril has, in fact, been the only one who hasn't pulled his weight; but as he's the legal owner and as his demands on the estate are as a rule relatively small, he's been left to do as he pleased and has no legitimate cause for complaint, in my professional opinion."

"And where did Aunt Adelaide come in?" Rhys asked.

"Nowhere, really. She was my wife's grandmother's sister. Since she had never married, she came here to be a sort of companion to Granny after their parents died and the home was broken up. She had a reasonable income of her own and could have supported herself somewhere else, but to the best of my knowledge nobody ever objected to her living here. There's plenty of room, obviously, and Addie was an easy person to get along with. I always thought Cyril seemed fond of his aunt, which shows the folly of judging by appearances."

"Oh, Lawrence, don't be so damned legal," snapped his wife. "Of course Cyril liked Aunt Addie. We all did. She was fun, with her present'ments and the way she'd grab at your sleeve and say 'Hark!' And she used to tell us stories and put stuff on our knees when we skinned them," Clara began to sniffle. "I don't know what possessed Cyril to act like that. He must have been out of his mind."

"Now, Clara."

Her husband began patting his wife's shoulder in the futile way men use when women cry.

"Clara's right," said May, not trying to be funny for once. "We all liked Aunt Addie much better than we did Granny. She was the one who'd write to us at school and sew on buttons and get cook to send us boxes of goodies, and she was never grouchy. Aunt Addie never had a cross word for anybody." She, too, began to sniffle.

"Inspector," evidently Squire had decided Rhys wasn't an honored guest any more, "you say my son evinced symptoms of having dosed himself with amphetamines. May one ask what those symptoms are?"

"Certainly. To begin with, there was his manic behavior during the mumming. He was constantly in motion, performing gyrations and acrobatics that were not only strange but downright dangerous for a man his age who doesn't look to be in top physical condition. He talked, sang, or shouted without stopping and without making much sense. He was contentious and insulting to yourself, whereas I had observed that your family are all accustomed to behaving toward you with respect and filial affection. According to what Lawrence has just said, the grievance he aired so loudly was no grievance at all. All these would be characteristic behavior patterns for an amphetamine user but not, I gather for Cyril. Do you agree?"

"I do."

"There were obvious physical symptoms as well. His pupils were contracted to pinpoints, whereas in the dim light everyone else's pupils had expanded as normal eyes always do. At dinner he ate nothing—amphetamines are appetite depressants, which explains their use in so-called diet pills—but drank a great deal, not only of wine but of whatever was available. Amphetamines make one extremely thirsty."

"God, yes," said Herbert. "He even asked for water. I never thought I'd live to see the day."

"But I thought speed really made you freak out," said Val.

"I mean, Uncle Cyril was acting crazy, but not so wild as—as some people I've heard about."

"I think that might be explained by your uncle's also having consumed a large amount of alcohol, which is a depressant. One could counteract the effects of the other to some extent. I should note that the scene culminating in your aunt's death occurred after he'd drunk a cup of hot coffee. Hot liquids give an extra kick to the effects of amphetamines. Cyril had been relatively quiescent at dinner because he was drinking so much wine."

"My God," said May. "I made him drink the coffee thinking it would sober him up. Instead it sent him into high gear again. Is that what you're saying?"

"That is what I'm theorizing, at any rate."

"But where would he get it?"

"It's around. Is Cyril in the habit of taking trips to Saint John, say, or Fredericton?"

"Cyril never goes anywhere if he can help it. He hasn't been off the place in ages."

"What does he do with his time?"

"He's supposed to be writing a book."

"What about?"

"Early lumbering in New Brunswick. That's how the Condryckes got started."

"Selling Crown lumber,"* somebody in the darkness muttered. Squire frowned and an awful silence descended.

"Go on," Rhys prodded. "Where does he get his reference material?"

"From local people, mostly. He's been collecting it for years."

"Gave him an excuse to hang around the rumshops and chin with the old souses," Herbert grunted.

---

* Crown lumber would have been timber marked, while still growing, by assigned agents for use by the Royal Navy. During the days of wooden ships, New Brunswick forests produced many of the tall, straight trees that were turned into masts and spars. To cut and sell any tree bearing the royal mark would, of course, have been an offense against the Crown.

"But he no longer does that?"

"Hell, no. He's one of the old souses himself."

"Judge not, Herb, lest you also be judged," Clara snapped. "Cyril's still our brother, I'll thank you to remember. Just because one of the staff slipped something into his drink . . ."

"One of the staff?" said Rhys. "Why would they do that?"

"Because they hate us, of course. They make believe they don't, but everybody knows they're all conspiring together to take over the country."

"And how would getting your brother Cyril high on speed assist the conspirators in taking over?"

Clara shrugged. "Don't ask me. It's like them, that's all."

"Clara, you must not make unsupported allegations," chided her husband. "That could be grounds for slander."

"I haven't named any names, have I? It's only slander if you name names."

"But do you in fact suspect any specific person?" Rhys insisted.

"How should I know? You're the detective. You find out."

"To do that I shall require your cooperation."

Rhys didn't put much stock in Clara's theory. Whatever their personal feelings about the Condryckes, the employees he'd seen so far at Graylings looked to be well kept, well fed, and no doubt as well paid as they were likely to be in that area. Of course the racial problem must exist to some extent here on the border between New Brunswick, which had been a Loyalist province although it was by now officially bilingual, and Quebec, the great enclave of the French. Maybe the staff did actively hate their employers. More likely, they regarded the Condryckes with amused contempt and instead of furiously coveting their substance, beguiled the long winter evenings thinking up more interesting ways to milk them out of it. Slaughtering geese that laid golden eggs had never been a generally popular sport among the thrifty, prudent Quebeçois. Still, one never knew.

"Does any of you know whether any member of the staff has any particular grudge against Cyril?"

"Like was he fooling around with somebody's wife or daughter?" Roy interjected to show he was on the ball and in there pitching.

"Hell, no," said Herbert. "Cyril talks a lot but he never does anything. Anyway, we've got a system around here. May deals with the inside staff. The outside men are responsible only to me. The rest of the family stay clear. Except Squire, of course, but he has his own duties and anyway he's the one who set the policy. The idea is to treat them just like any factory hand or whatever with a certain job to do, instead of servants who are at everybody's beck and call. That way we eliminate friction. We pay them well, provide comfortable quarters for times like now when they can't get back and forth to their own homes, and don't interfere with their off hours or butt into their personal affairs."

"That sounds like an excellent system," said Rhys.

"It's worked so far. At least we keep the same people, and they do a good job for us. The only one who comes in contact with the whole family as a rule is Ludovic, and he's British so he understands what service is all about. As far as I know he gets along with the house staff. May would hear about it fast enough if he didn't. I'm sorry, Clara, but I don't see where your idea can hold water."

"You haven't proved anything," his sister-in-law argued. "You say everything is hearts and flowers with the staff, but that doesn't make it so. You don't know everything that goes on."

Rhys had heard enough bickering. "Thank you, Clara. I shall be able to find out what I need to know."

"How, for instance?"

"That is a professional secret."

"Hey, none of that rubber hose stuff like they have in the States," cried Herbert.

"Rubber hoses are not part of our official equipment,"

Rhys assured him. "My methods are quite painless and usually effective. Your staff will not quit in righteous indignation and none of you will be incommoded any more than is necessary. Rest assured, I do not wish to bite the hands that have so lavishly fed me. Unless it were to become necessary in self-defense." Rhys preferred not to make promises he might have to break.

Val emitted a nervous giggle. "I must say, Mama, you know how to pick 'em. Whatever possessed you to invite a Mountie?"

"Naturally your mother didn't know," Donald told her in a hurt, dignified tone that must mean he was beside himself with fury. "Lady Rhys deceived us."

"Donald, I don't think that's very courteous of you," said his wife. "Please remember that Lady Rhys is a valued acquaintance of ours, as are Sir Emlyn and Dafydd. We invited Madoc and Janet out of respect for his family and because we thought another young couple would be fun for Val and Roy. Furthermore, I personally am more than grateful Madoc is with us now. Hasn't it occurred to anybody but myself that I could be in a very precarious position if he weren't around?"

"Precarious?" said her husband. "Babs, what are you talking about?"

"Quite simply, Donald, I was the only one out there with Cyril when Aunt Addie was freezing to death outside. It's only my word against his, assuming he were coherent enough to talk, that I didn't push her out myself."

"But that's absurd. Why would you?"

"Naturally I wouldn't, but you know what the local people might think, and where it might lead. Quite frankly, I wish you'd be a little less hostile to Madoc, because I'm depending on him to keep me out of jail."

CHAPTER 15

"I've been wondering," said Lawrence, "when someone other than myself was going to think of that."

"Lawrence, how could you?" cried his wife. "You know Babs would never . . ."

"My dear, I know nothing of the sort. I surmise Babs would not kill Aunt Addie because she's a sensible woman who isn't apt to go off half-cocked. She's always appeared fond of Addie, as we all were, and I can't think offhand why she'd want to murder her. However, that's only my assumption. When it comes to physical proof that Babs could not have committed the act, I think I can do a little better."

"How?" said Rhys. "Did you happen to see what actually happened?"

"I did not. My proof is circumstantial but, I think, conclusive enough. Clara, would you oblige me by going out in the hall and opening the front door?"

"You mean right now? With this gale blowing?"

"This is the same gale that was blowing when Aunt Addie was thrust out into the snow, is it not?"

"Well, yes, of course."

"Wind's gone down a little, I think," said Herbert.

"Good. This should make the test that much more effective. Clara, would you mind?"

"Wait a second," said Roy. "What about fingerprints on the doorknob, eh?"

"They wouldn't prove anything," Herbert reminded him. "We were all pawing at the knob trying to get Aunt Addie inside. Go ahead, Clara. I think I see what Lawrence is driving at."

"But why me? Why not May?"

"Because you're just about the same size and weight as Babs. Come on, let's get it over with."

"This isn't one of your crazy jokes? You're not going to slam the door and leave me out there?"

"Clara, I think we're all agreed that the time for crazy jokes is past."

Squire sounded exhausted and probably was. "Please do as Lawrence says. I'm sure you're as anxious as the rest of us to clear Babs of any possible suspicion, not that we . . ."

He shook his head and sighed. Clara went out to the door, not at all happy, and the rest trooped behind her.

"Madoc, you stand right here beside me. I've known this lot too long." Clara gritted her teeth and took hold of the great iron handle.

"Well, come on, Clara, open it," May cried impatiently.

"I can't. It won't budge."

Clara put her shoulder against the door and shoved with all her might. The shoulder seam of the flapper dress she was still wearing split from the strain, but the door held.

"Can't do it, eh?" said Lawrence. "Val, you're young and strong. You try."

Val took Clara's place with no better luck.

"Show her how, Roy," said Lawrence.

"It does open out and not in, right? I mean, they're not pushing when they ought to be pulling?"

"Oh, no. The door opens outward in order to display the very handsome wrought iron hinges to better advantage. Open it, please."

Roy flexed his muscles, turned the knob, and pushed. He pushed harder. Sweat stood out on his forehead. At last he managed to push the door open a crack. At once the wind snatched the massive oaken slab, flapped it open and slammed it back, almost taking his arm off before he could get it out of the way.

"There, see." Lawrence had reason to be proud of his demonstration. "Now if you'll kindly tell me how Babs could have got that door open with a seventy-mile gale blowing against it and managed to hold it with one hand long enough to shove Aunt Addie out with the other, I'll eat my Sunday boots. I rest my case."

"Clara," said Babs with a choke in her voice, "do you mind if I kiss your husband?"

"God, I'd kiss him, too, if I dared." Donald heaved a mighty sigh of relief. "Satisfied now, Rhys?"

"Oh, yes. Thank you very much."

"I'll bet I could open it," said May.

"The hell you could," her husband retorted. "What if the wind dragged you out there and slammed the door shut and we couldn't get to you fast enough? Christ, haven't we got enough corpses around this house already?"

"Then how could Cyril do it?"

"Because Cyril's a man, for one thing, and men are stronger than women. He also weighs maybe fifty pounds more than you do. He was high on some damn thing or other and people in that state do things they could never do when they were in their right minds. Remember how he hung by his hands and did a back flip over the banisters when we were coming down the stairs? Ever known him to pull a stunt like that before?"

"He used to do it when we were kids."

"How many years ago was that?" said Lawrence.

"All right, Lawrence, I get your point. You'd rather hang my brother than my sister-in-law."

"May, I don't want to hang anybody, that's just the point. We can all testify Cyril wasn't in his right mind. Rhys says he'd been taking drugs. If he took them knowingly, I suppose he's in for it; but if he didn't, then I'm sure we can do something for him. It could have been an accident, a mistake. It could have been vindictiveness on the part of some of the staff. I'm not ruling that out even if Herb and you are. Cyril could make himself damned obnoxious when he had a skinful and thought he was being funny. The gist of it is, I can probably do something for Cyril. I couldn't do a damn thing for Babs. I'm saying this in front of Rhys because he couldn't possibly be stupid enough to draw the wrong conclusion on the strength of the evidence. Don't ask me why Cyril shoved Aunt Addie out the door. I assume it was because of the fire ship and the fact that she'd given him a scolding. What he did was childish and unspeakably rude, but it wouldn't have been dangerous under ordinary circumstances."

"If it were, Don and I would have been dead long ago," said Clara. "Cyril was always doing it to us when we were little. Remember, Don? He'd say, 'This is my house and I can put you out any time I want to.' And May would get furious and tell him to shut up."

"I'm glad you remembered that, Clara," said Squire. "As you see, Inspector Rhys, my daughter has just given you proof that I'd never concealed his status as titular head of the house from Cyril, even when he was a boy. His rage against me this afternoon could not have had any rational basis. You may be all wrong about that drug business, Rhys. You're no doctor. Cyril may have had a brainstorm of some kind and thought he was a boy again. Though why he turned on his own father I can't imagine."

The reigning monarch had been reduced to a fretful old man. "I always thought we got on well enough."

"Anyway, Cyril always let us in again," Donald said loyally. "He didn't mean anything by shutting us out. He just wanted to show who was boss."

"Then if I hadn't come along and made a scene, he'd probably have let Aunt Addie back in." Babs wrung her hands. "All I did was get his back up by trying to make him do what he'd meant to do anyway. So—so I suppose I killed her, after all."

"Nonsense," May bellowed. "You did no such thing. Anybody would have done what you did. Nobody could hold you responsible. Could they, Lawrence?"

"Positively not. You can't try a case on the basis of what might have been. Rhys will bear me out on that, I trust."

"Besides," said Roy, who must still have hopes, "if Cyril was on speed as Rhys says, he'd forgotten she was there, like as not. At least your aunt would have stood some kind of chance if he'd opened the door when you told him to."

"Roy's right, Mama," Val chimed in. "Anyway, the person really responsible is the one who slipped Uncle Cyril the speed, if you ask me."

Babs was still wringing those hands of hers, capable hands that must be used to dealing effectively with any problem that came their way. "You're sweet to try to make me feel better, darlings, but I suppose I'll always feel I should have handled the situation more intelligently. As to how Cyril might have got hold of reducing pills, I can't imagine. One would think that was the last thing on earth he'd bother with. May, can you think of anything?"

Interesting that Babs asked May. Was she trying to divert attention from Val, who might very well have done a little experimenting with pill-popping? Did Babs know or suspect what had been going on in the billiard room?

Franny and Winny were trying ever so hard not to look at each other, Rhys noted. He'd tackle that pair when he could get them alone. They'd be too smart or too scared to give a coherent answer in front of the assembled clan.

May couldn't think of anything, or claimed she couldn't. Either she was a remarkably obtuse mother or an overprotective one. Rhys felt like telling her to smarten up. Instead he went doggedly on with his questions.

"If Cyril had no friendly contact with any of the servants and hadn't been off the place in months, that means one of yourselves is the likeliest person to have got the drug for him. You're quite sure nobody has anything further to tell me? He hasn't asked any of you to fill a prescription or pick up a package for him, for instance? You could have done it in all innocence, you know."

Squire appointed himself spokesman for that one. "The suggestion that Cyril hasn't been off the place for months may be open to question, Inspector. We're a busy family and we don't sit in each other's pockets all the time. Clara and Lawrence only come for weekends and holidays as a rule, Donald and Babs can't be with us as often as we'd like, and Val and the boys are still at school. Herbert, May, and I all have reason to leave the place from time to time. May and Clara went on a Christmas shopping spree to Montreal a week ago, for instance. I was in Fredericton on business for the estate last Tuesday and Wednesday. Herbert drove down to pick up the boys day before yesterday. This is typical of our behavior pattern. Cyril might easily have decided to drive into Charlo or somewhere without bothering to mention it. As long as he was back in time for dinner, it's unlikely anybody would notice. As to how he might have obtained drugs on any such excursion, I expect you could answer better than I. From what one reads in the papers, it would appear these things are readily available."

"One would have to know where to look, however," said Rhys. "A respectably dressed, middle-aged man asking at random where he might purchase narcotics would be apt to get taken for an underground government agent doing a remarkably stupid job of investigation."

"Why the hell should Cyril start looking for dope anyway?" Herbert broke in. "Cyril's not a drug addict, he's a soak. Don't glare at me, Squire. We all know Cy drinks from the time he gets up in the morning till he keels over for the night. We also know there's not a damn thing we can do to stop him, so we don't try. What the hell, the rest of us like our cup o' tea, too, though we don't overdo it as he does. Anyway, Rhys, what I'm getting at is that Cyril likes booze and he can always find plenty of it right here at Graylings. Why should he risk his neck and freeze his ass off humping over the road looking for something to get high on when he's high as a kite already? Answer me that one, will you?"

"Herbert, you might have had sense enough to keep your foot out of your mouth," snarled Clara. "Squire just got the rest of us off the hook and now you've stuck us right back on again. I've always said May was a fool to marry you."

"That so? Then I've been a damn sight kinder to you than you have to me, Clara. Want me to go into particulars in front of Lawrence?"

"Shut up, you two," May barked. "If there was ever a time when a family should stick together, this is it. I don't know what we're standing around here spouting this nonsense for in the first place. All we have to do is wait till Cyril wakes up and ask him where he got whatever it was he took."

"Huh!" snorted her younger sister. "Do you think he'll tell you?"

"He'd better. He knows what will happen to him if he doesn't."

"What will happen?" Rhys asked.

"Oh, May has her own little ways of putting a man through hell if he doesn't toe the line," the loquacious Herbert replied. "His socks don't match, his bed gets lumps in it, he always winds up with the piece of meat that's all fat, he can't sit down without a draft on the back of his neck. Yes, sirree Bob, when it comes to driving a man nuts, my little Maysie's got 'em all beat hands down."

Little Maysie replied that ol' Herb was no slouch at it, either. "Anyway, Madoc, you just wait. I promise you faithfully I'll get it out of him first thing in the morning, one way or another. And I'll bet you five dollars it'll turn out some floozy in a bar somewhere sold him the dope as a virility pill and he's been hanging onto it in case some cute little trick like Janet happened along."

Janet took that remark none too kindly. "I can't imagine

why he'd bother. He has no cause to suppose I'd be interested."

"Hell," said Herbert, "that wouldn't stop him. If Cyril could think straight, he'd lay off the hooch once in a while. Then maybe he wouldn't need to be taking stuff in the first place."

"Does Cyril in fact take aphrodisiacs?" Rhys insisted.

"Not to my knowledge. We were kidding about it the other day, that's all. He said he hadn't been able to—I shouldn't be saying these things in front of the kids."

"They could no doubt tell you a few things," snorted his wife with a glance at Val. "Madoc, for heaven's sake, it's Christmas Eve. Do we have to go on and on about this awful thing? Why don't we just get poor old Aunt Addie upstairs, then sing a few carols—religious ones, you know, like 'Silent Night'—and maybe have a little nightcap and go to bed?"

"I can't say I feel much like singing Christmas carols," Babs replied in an exhausted voice, "but I should most awfully like to have a good, hot soak in a bathtub and then go straight to bed. I'm sure Cyril didn't realize how hard he was hitting me with that cane."

"Good Lord, Babs, do you think he broke something?" cried her distraught husband. "Where does it hurt?"

"Right now I simply ache all over. Please, Inspector, couldn't we leave the rest of it till morning as May suggests? I assure you we're none of us going anywhere in this storm."

"Have to be crazy to try," Lawrence grunted. "What do you say, Rhys?"

"Yes, why not? I think we have accomplished all we can with this discussion. Roy and Herbert, perhaps you might carry Miss Adelaide's body upstairs and put her in the same room with her sister. I shall remain downstairs in case anybody might like a word with me in private. Janet will also stay, in her capacity as note-taker. If you don't mind, Jenny," the Mountie added with his most wistfully pleading smile.

"I don't want to leave you, Madoc. Maybe Franny and Winny would like to have first crack at a private talk with you. I can tell they're itching to get into a huddle with a real, live detective."

That was a lie pure and simple. Franny and Winny were no doubt wetting their pants at the prospect, but they wouldn't dare say so. Janet had all the instincts of a policeman's wife, bless her resourceful little heart.

"All right, you two," said Herbert, "but make it short and cut along to bed right afterward. This isn't the sort of treat your mother and I had in mind for you, but you might as well enjoy it if you can. We'll find a way to make things up to you somehow."

"Don't worry, Dad. We're okay. You'd better get some sleep yourself."

Franny was by far the more self-possessed of the two. Winny was trying hard to emulate his brother's coolness, but making a poor fist of it. As Roy and Herbert were preparing to move the blanket-wrapped body from the chesterfield, Ludovic, who had remained discreetly absent until now, manifested himself.

"Will there be anything else tonight, sir?"

"I think not," said Squire. "I doubt if anybody wants to sing carols, May, and I for one have no interest in a nightcap, except to cover my old bald head. The family will be going to bed, Ludovic. Inspector Rhys will stay down here for a while."

Squire took it for granted the butler would require no explanation. Ludovic didn't even nod.

"I have opened the damper in the library stove, sir. Perhaps Inspector Rhys would prefer to sit in there."

"Thank you, Ludovic. That would be more comfortable." At last he was going to have a chance to do what the real detectives did, though probably little would come of it. "Shall we go to the library, boys?"

Rhys didn't have to ask Janet her preference. The Great

Hall was arctic now that the wind had picked up again, the fire was down, and the thermometer must be hovering well below minus thirty. That thermal underwear with its tinsel trimming couldn't be doing his affianced bride much good. He put his arm around her and squeezed her as tight as was consistent with locomotion as they walked together away from the departing Condryckes.

CHAPTER 16

"Ludovic, would there be a cup of hot tea going? I think Miss Wadman could use one. So could I, for that matter. How about you lads? By tea I mean, of course, tea," Rhys added and Winny looked around as if for a chance to escape.

"We never touch the stuff," Franny said with a swagger that might have deceived himself but not anyone else.

Ludovic went out of the library, still impeccably deadpan, and Rhys got down to work.

"Now would you two care to tell me what it was you fed your Uncle Cyril this afternoon?"

"Us? We never gave him anything. What makes you think we're into speed?" Franny protested.

"Well, you do toss around expressions like speed as if they weren't totally unfamiliar to you. And there is the fact that you've been high on pot ever since Miss Wadman and I arrived at Graylings. Where do you get it?"

"We don't know what you're talking about," Winny tried to insist.

"Come off it, young man. You're not talking to your doting and innocent parents now. I do have a nose, fairly sharp eyes, and far too much experience with silly young chaps like you. You've been smoking in the billiard room. You had one last night and you shared a joint right after lunch today."

"Get him!" cried Franny. "The big detective. How the hell would you know we had one right after lunch?"

"Elementary, my dear jughead. Lunch was very late today on account of the conference among your elders. You were in reasonable shape then. At approximately three o'clock pip

emma, when Miss Wadman and I were forced in from a walk
by a snow squall, we wound up in the hallway that leads past
the billiard room. We smelled pot and heard you talking. You
were totally spaced-out and talking a bunch of sickening rot
that no doubt struck you at the time as brilliant. Your eyes
were still red when you appeared in your lobster suits later,
but your brains were somewhat less addled. You haven't been
at it long, have you? Otherwise you'd have known enough to
open the windows and do something about your eyes. Not a
remarkably good show, all in all. To rephrase my earlier
question, where did you get it?"

"At school," Franny mumbled.

"From whom?"

"A kid."

"What kid?"

"John Smith."

"Come off it."

Franny shrugged. "That's what he calls himself."

"Is he a student at the school?"

"No."

"If you'd talk a little faster, we could get this over sooner.
Who is he, then?"

"I don't know. He's just a guy who comes around and the
kids buy off him."

"What do they buy?"

"Pot, mostly. I guess."

"And what did you buy?"

"A nickel bag."

"By which I assume you mean five dollars' worth, right?"

"Yeah. Five was all we had. Winny and I'd been buying
presents for the family, see?"

"How noble of you. How often do you make your buys
from this alleged John Smith?"

"This was our first time. We just thought it would be something to do up here."

"To take your minds off the joyous merrymakings?"

"It's such a drag."

Franny made the pronouncement in the tone of a world-weary roué. "The same damn stuff every year, and we're supposed to make believe we're having a ball so Squire won't go into one of his fits. How much can you take, eh?"

"What sorts of fits does Squire go into?"

"Oh, you know. Huffs around and sulks and says he's going to cut off our allowances because we're a pack of ingrates."

"Squire pays your allowances?"

"How could he cut them if he didn't?" Winny asked logically enough.

"Doesn't your father get a salary for his work as steward?"

"Well, that's an allowance, sort of, isn't it? I mean, Squire doesn't have to keep Dad on here if he doesn't want to. At least he's said so often enough. Granny used to shut him up and say she was the boss here, not Squire, but I don't know if she meant it or was just being nasty. Anyway, she's gone now so you'd have thought Squire was boss, but now Uncle Cyril says he is. Only Uncle Cyril's going to jail, isn't he? What's going to happen?"

"Time will tell," said Rhys.

"You're not going to rat on us?"

"About smoking pot? How much do you have left?"

"None," mumbled Franny. "That was our last joint we smoked this afternoon."

"Did you enjoy it?"

"Yeah, sure. I guess. I don't remember very well."

"Rather a stupid way to blow five dollars, then, wasn't it? You'd have done better to buy comic books, since you appear inclined toward infantile pastimes."

"What do you mean, infantile?"

"Sticking something in your mouth and sucking on it. Reducing yourself to the state of a baby who can't even talk straight so that you can swank around in front of a bunch of other nitwits who don't know what's going on, either. This John Smith is either another sucker like yourselves with a habit to support or else he's trying to make suckers out of you. When you get back to school, someone from the local police will be in touch with you about John Smith. You will keep your mouths shut and cooperate. Is that fully understood? If you'd prefer, I can haul you in and let you think about it."

"You don't give us much choice, do you?"

"I'm giving you a chance to save your necks and you'll be smart to take it. What did you buy your Uncle Cyril for Christmas?"

"A book," Franny replied. "We always get him a book. That way we can put it on his charge account and he never knows the difference."

"The true Yuletide spirit. Where is the book now?"

"Under the tree with the rest of the presents, I guess. We got Val to wrap it for us."

"Nice of her. What did you get Val?"

"Sort of a—a joke thing."

"Such as what?"

"Well, they had these bikini things with sayings on them. We just sort of thought it would be something Val would get a bang out of."

"Yeah, Val always gets a bang out of her bikinis," Winny giggled.

Janet primmed her mouth. "Madoc, how much of this am I supposed to be taking down?"

"Just that reminder about getting the police on to John Smith. Unless there's something else these jolly boys would like to tell me, such as what Smith sells besides pot."

"We wouldn't know," Franny insisted. "Honest, Inspector, we never made but that one buy, and we had to get one of the other guys who's a regular customer to do it for us. We couldn't even tell you what John Smith looks like. We've only seen him from a distance."

"Don't push it, Franny. I expect your memory will improve once you get back to school and have your little session with your friendly neighborhood fuzz. Run along to bed now, children. Ah, Ludovic, good timing."

"I regret the delay, sir. The kitchen staff had retired and it was necessary to boil up a fresh kettle."

"No matter, you're just in time. Sit down and chat a bit. Jenny darling, you won't mind if Ludovic and I happen to lapse into our native tongue on occasion?"

"Not at all. It will give me a chance to get used to the sound. Set that tray in front of me, Ludovic, and park yourself in the easy chair over there. You might just poke another stick into the stove on your way past, if you feel you've got to earn your keep. I don't dare ask Madoc for fear he'll put me behind bars."

In a moment the three of them were toasting themselves most agreeably around the roaring stove, sipping the tea Janet poured out. This was the way to treat a Welshman no matter what his position, because there has never been a Welshman alive who has not known himself to be the equal of anybody and maybe a little more equal than some and be damned to them all though it would not be sound politics to say so. Ludovic the perfect butler, Ludovic the probable crook, became simply Ludovic, chatting with a knight's son and receiving hospitality from the hand of the son's lovely bride-to-be.

Perhaps the man was feeling a gentle melancholy that Janet's loveliness could never be his to possess, but that would be part of the pleasure. Yearning for that which could never be attained was what made the Welsh bards such great poets. Being a cop and not a bard, Madoc spent a moment in silent rejoicing that his own satisfaction was within the price of a license, then got down to business.

"This has not been a typical Christmas Eve at Graylings would you say, Ludovic?"

"It has not, sir. I fear you and Miss Wadman will carry away no favorable impression to your distinguished parents. Squire will take that hard. He has been dreaming of having

Sir Emlyn and perchance even Sir Caradoc under his roof one day."

"Janet and I were not invited for our wit and charm alone?"

"Not you, sir."

Janet gave the butler a look over the rim of her teacup. "Ludovic, how do the Condryckes feel about Val's romance with Roy Robbins?"

"They hope it will be of short duration, miss."

"Would Donald by any chance have got wind of the fact that Roy was chasing me around the typewriters not too long ago?"

"Mr. Donald takes a paternal interest in the company's employees."

"So the idea was that I should tumble back into Roy's everloving arms as soon as he made another pass at me, which Donald knew he would because that's the way Roy is. Val would then be able to get in her licks with Madoc, since she'd fluffed it with the elder brother, right?"

"They felt it was worth a shot, miss."

Madoc cleared his throat. "As a matter of passing interest, so to speak, has Roy in fact made another pass at you?"

"Ask Ludovic," Janet replied demurely.

"Mr. Robbins is exhibiting toward Miss Wadman the manner of a young man who has had his ears pinned back good and proper, sir."

Rhys laughed. "We seem to have been a complete bust all around. Any more tea in the pot, love?"

"Pass your cup."

Ludovic made no effort to assist in this small task, perhaps because he considered himself off-duty, perhaps because he divined that Madoc would use the excuse to sneak in a mildly surreptitious caress, which in fact was the case.

"How does the kitchen feel about the Donalds and Val?" Rhys asked when he'd got himself untangled and his cup refilled.

"As Squire explained earlier, there is little exchange between the staff and the nonresident members of the family. By and large, Mr. and Mrs. Donald are thought to be harmless enough. Miss Val is the subject of some discussion. The maid who does her room considers her lazy and untidy. Her relationships with the young men she brings up here have given rise to considerable ribaldry during the past few years. There is the feeling among some of the male employees that Miss Val could, as the saying is, be had but would not be worth the effort."

Rhys's wistful brown eyes turned involuntarily to his own ladylove. Ludovic noticed and smiled.

"Miss Wadman is in great favor with the staff. Her demeanor in the kitchen and her idiomatic command of the French tongue made a favorable impression on Fifine, the cook, who is a woman of power. Admiration was warmly expressed among the males, but the consensus is that a man would have to be *folle à la tête* to trifle with the affianced bride of Detective Inspector Madoc Rhys."

"They know who I am?" said Rhys sharply.

"The information did not come from me, sir. After your capture of Mad Carew the Murdering Maniac of the Mirimachi, you are something of a legend in these parts. Is it true, sir, that you tracked that man of fiendish cunning and titanic strength one hundred twenty-seven miles through unbroken wilderness, armed only with a slingshot against a throwing knife, a double-bitted axe, and a high-powered hunting rifle?"

"The slingshot is apocryphal," Rhys answered, greatly embarrassed by this adulation of a task that had been considered merely a routine assignment back at headquarters. "We are not supposed to rely on force of arms but on force of character. I just tagged along till Carew had got a blister on his heel and a fuzzy caterpillar down his back, then slipped the cuffs on him while he was resting his foot and trying to dislodge the bug. The hardest part was trying to read him his rights. I had to get the caterpillar out before he'd listen to me. You will please inform those lecherous hounds out there, however, that I am indeed a man to be reckoned with where my Janet is concerned. What's the scuttlebutt on Clara and Lawrence?"

"Mrs. Clara is sometimes inclined to meddle. Mr. Lawrence is considered to have done himself well in marrying her and thus securing the large business connected with the Condrycke interests."

"Does he have much other business?"

"I believe not. Most folk in these parts prefer to employ a French lawyer."

"The Lawrences are at Graylings a great deal, are they not?"

"Far too often, in the opinions of the staff."

"What do you think?"

Ludovic shrugged. "I should say Mrs. Clara wishes she were in her sister's shoes, and possibly vice versa. Clara envies May her position as mistress of Graylings. I suspect May sometimes envies Clara's being able to come here and enjoy the amenities, then go away and leave May stuck with the responsibility. Her position is a confining one, as you must realize, despite its many perquisites."

"Squire expects a lot of May, does he?"

"Squire is an autocrat. He is an intelligent man who gave up whatever other opportunities he might have had to marry Miss Dorothy and settle down at Graylings, so he has funneled all his talent and ambition into making a success of the venture, and he has succeeded. He has, I may say, more brains than any of his children. His is the brain that controls Donald's activities in the company. He is quite aware of Donald's limitations."

"What are they?"

"Charm of manner, a good memory, an ability to look intelligent, and a marked lack of practical acumen. Donald is what is known, I believe, as a front man."

"That doesn't surprise me," said Janet. "Somebody once

told me," it had been Roy but she needn't go into that, "Mr. Condrycke was the one they depended on to keep the customers' wives happy. I assume that means he and Babs handle the entertainment part, giving dinners and so forth. Do they bring people to Graylings much?"

"Often. Squire relies on Donald for distinguished company."

"And other things." Janet smiled. "Too bad I let him down."

"Only in one respect, miss. As a prospective member of the Rhys family, you would have been welcome in any case. Squire likes being surrounded by celebrities and persons of rank. Your name will no doubt be mentioned on any number of occasions, though your husband's profession may not."

"Well, I'm used to being talked about. In Pitcherville it happens to everybody. By now Sam Neddick must have told the whole town Janet Wadman's fixed it up with that Mountie who pinched him in Moose Jaw."

Her imitation of her brother's hired man wasn't too far off the mark. "They must be taking bets already about when the baby's due. It's going to come as a nasty shock to the ladies down at the Tuesday Club when they find out we haven't jumped the gun."

Ludovic laughed outright. He said something in Welsh and Madoc laughed, too.

"I'd better not translate that. She blushes easily. Getting back to Squire, any idea where he came from?"

"His origins are shrouded in obscurity, sir. By now, in my opinion, he's managed to convince himself he is in truth a Condrycke. I have sometimes wondered whether he might once have been a member of a traveling theatrical company."

"His penchant for pageantry?"

"Precisely, sir. I should venture to guess that he invests the role of squire with a good deal more grandeur than would be found, for instance, in your own family."

"You wouldn't be far wrong. My father's about as awesome as a church mouse and my great-uncle is often mistaken for one of his own sheepmen. Squire must indeed be an able manager if he can handle a complexity of business interests and remember to be impressive at the same time. Does he ever slip? When one of his playful offspring is putting a rubber lizard down his back, for instance?"

"Putting rubber lizards down Squire's back is not the done thing, sir. Mr. Cyril's antics this evening were the first episode of anyone's making sport of Squire that I can recall. I am bound to say that Squire handled the situation with a greater degree of tolerance than I should have expected."

"What might he otherwise have done?"

"Thrown a temperament, which he manages with truly frightening dramatic effect, and banish Cyril from the revels."

"Assuming that Cyril had not been suffering from a temporary mental aberration brought about, in my opinion, by the ingestion of drugs, would Cyril have allowed himself to be banished?"

"It has happened before, sir, though Mrs. May and Mr. Herbert are usually able to handle him well enough as they did at luncheon today, merely by letting him get drunk to the point of incapability. Mr. Cyril is not as a rule a boisterous drunk. His temperament leans more to the phlegmatic than the choleric."

"You've never before seen him act as he did tonight?"

"Never, sir."

"What did you think about it?"

"I thought Herbert's lads had slipped something into his drink."

"You know what they've been up to, then?"

"It's part of my job to know what people are up to at Graylings, sir. And to keep my mouth shut about it, which I should normally do. You no doubt realize that I'm laying my job on the line by talking to you in this way. I am supposed to represent the feudal element among the paid help," Ludovic added in a totally human tone.

"Your feudality is safe with Jenny and me, as you made

damn sure it would be before you opened up," Rhys answered. "Are they all in bed."

"As to that I could not say, sir. The family are somewhat addicted to holding private conferences in each other's bedrooms. I should venture to speculate that a certain amount of tiptoeing back and forth is still taking place."

"We had some of that last night, too," said Janet, cutting another sliver of fruitcake.

Ludovic was amused. "Miss Val's having a thin time of it this trip. I trust you were not seriously incommoded, Miss Wadman?"

"It wasn't the sort of thing I've been brought up to expect in decent people's houses," she replied in that prissy little way that so delighted her husband-to-be. "Back home it only happens in haylofts when the girl's none too bright and the man's none too particular. Maybe you'd better make up a bed for Madoc on the chesterfield here in case I have to evict him again."

"I doubt I shall be sleeping much tonight," said Rhys. "If I do, I shall lie across my Jenny's threshold like a Russian serf in the time of the czars. Why do you think old Mrs. Condrycke was murdered, Ludovic?"

CHAPTER 17

"I beg your pardon, sir. Miss Adelaide was not a Condrycke. Her family name was Stebbins."

"Thank you, but I am not referring to Miss Adelaide Stebbins. I meant her sister Rosa, who predeceased her by, I should say, just about twenty-four hours."

"But Mrs. Condrycke—you—you did say murdered, sir?"

"The evidence indicates that Mrs. Rosa Stebbins Condrycke was assisted to her demise by violent methods."

Ludovic was visibly rattled. "Is it permitted to ask by what methods, sir?"

"I should say she was smothered with a wet towel or something of the sort while under the influence of that pitcherful of wassail you took up to her."

"Then you're accusing me of . . ." Ludovic swallowed hard.

"Should I? You didn't, did you?"

"I'm not a complete fool, sir."

"I didn't think you were. That's why my Janet is pouring your tea. As a matter of professional curiosity, what were you sent up for?"

"Forgery, sir. I got into a spot of bother with the bookmakers. I was only a footman at the time," Ludovic added by way of excuse. "Unfortunately, my then employer was in very deep water himself just then. My dipping into his bank account interfered with an elaborate system of check kiting he'd worked quite successfully for some while. He naturally welcomed the opportunity to cover his own maneuverings by accusing me of grand larceny. Being a sporting man himself, he then offered to rig an escape for me, thus allegedly confirming my guilt and getting him off the hook while saving myself a longish holiday at Her Majesty's expense.

"He provided me with a forged passport and a ticket to Canada. I wrote myself some excellent references promoting myself to butler and obtained this post at Graylings. My intention was to move on once my credibility had been established, but as you see, I never did. The pay is excellent, the work is not arduous by and large, and, *entre nous,* some of the ladies in the area are most obliging."

"But don't you miss your family back in Wales?" cried Janet.

"I had not been in contact with them for some years prior to my abrupt emigration. I had run away from home at twelve to avoid going down into the mines. As there were at least eleven other children at the time, I doubt whether my parents ever noticed my absence. I order gift packages to be sent them from time to time, but as circumstances prevent my enclosing a return name and address they never know where to reply and probably don't much care."

"The warrant for your arrest has no doubt expired some time ago," said Rhys. "I'm sure you could return unchallenged if you so desired."

Ludovic shrugged. "Perhaps I will, someday."

"If you care to give me a name and address, I will have discreet inquiries made."

"Thank you." The butler didn't sound overcome by gratitude. "I suppose it would be as well to know whether anybody is left to receive my packages."

Janet shivered and Rhys noticed.

"Tired, my darling?"

"Not particularly. Maybe a goose walked over my grave. Life's a complicated business, isn't it? That's a trite and silly thing to say."

Janet straightened up and adjusted her skirt. "Why don't

you tell us who killed Mrs. Condrycke, Ludovic, so we can all get some sleep?"

"I should be more than willing to tell you if I knew," the ex-forger replied. "It is shocking to me that such a thing can have happened here without my knowing."

He rose and returned the empty teacups to the tray, as if to reassure himself that he was still able to function. "May one ask, Inspector, whether your presence here is an indication that you anticipated some such occurrence?"

"You may ask, but the answer is no. Our coming is simply a result of my mother's never-flagging urge to make cozy arrangements for people. I had never met any of the Condryckes till the night Donald and Babs asked us up here, and it appears Donald knew more about Janet than she did about him."

"At least Donald and Babs couldn't have been planning to kill Granny if they invited strangers into the house for the purpose of separating Val from Roy," said Janet. "Don't you think that lets them off the hook?"

"Never let anyone off the hook till you've got somebody else safe in the net," Rhys answered. "That's what we learn in detective school, love."

"Sounds like some of the neighbors back in Pitcherville. Guilty till proven innocent and even so there's no smoke without fire. You were just lucky enough to get away with it and you needn't think you can pull the wool over their eyes because they know better. All right, then. Donald's guilty, so is Babs, and everybody else is even guiltier. I'll take Roy for a starter. Since he probably never set eyes on Granny alive, he's sure to be the likeliest suspect."

"And his motive?"

"Easy. He wants to marry into the firm and Granny was out to put a spoke into his wheel because she didn't think he was good enough for Val."

"Do you?"

"They look to me like two peas in a pod."

"Is Roy capable at his job?"

"So-so. He's clever enough, I suppose, but he's inclined to be lazy. The secretaries have been covering for him because he butters them up, but his charm's begun to wear thin in spots. I think he might be good at the public relations stuff, like Donald. And I noticed Val started being awfully sweet to Uncle Cyril once she found out he holds the purse strings, or thinks he does, so I suppose she could do the same with the big butter-and-egg men from Manitoba. What do you think, Ludovic? Am I just being catty because Val dresses better than I do?"

"That is open to dispute, Miss Wadman. I have not seen you other than appropriately and attractively dressed. Miss Val is inclined to err on the side of fashion as opposed to taste, as she has perhaps done with Mr. Robbins. In fairness to that young man, I do not see how he can have become a serious bone of contention between her and her grandmother, although Mrs. Condrycke did in fact meet him at tea the day he arrived. As far as I could see, they got along well enough. Mr. Robbins is only one in a long string of suitors Miss Val has brought here, and Mrs. Condrycke was more amused than annoyed by them, as a rule. Only a couple of months ago, Miss Val was crowing that she was virtually engaged to the distinguished tenor, Mr. Dafydd Rhys."

"Many young women have made the same mistake," said Madoc. "By now, Dafydd has probably forgotten her name, if in fact he ever remembered. He writes them on his shirt cuffs to remind him, usually. By the time his laundry is done, so is the romance."

"I must remember to keep writing my name on your cuffs," Janet observed.

"And I must remember not to let my brother borrow my shirts. How did Val get on with Granny, by and large?"

"As well as could be expected, sir. The late Mrs. Condrycke was not a particularly amiable old lady, and sometimes diverted herself by encouraging Miss Val's more outrageous antics while her parents were endeavoring to restrain her. On the other hand, Mrs. Condrycke scorned the laxity of the modern generation. To be sure, she scorned every other generation, including her own."

"Did she have any special animosity toward Val's parents?"

"When it came to animosity, Mrs. Condrycke did not play favorites. She thought Donald a fool and Cyril a sot, Lawrence a pettifogging bootlicker, and Herbert a glad-hander with an eye to the main chance. She frequently berated May and Clara for letting themselves be taken in."

"What about Babs?"

"She had a grudging respect for Mrs. Donald. She once asked why Mrs. Babs hadn't held out for a better offer."

"And what did Babs say to that?"

"She said, 'Hasn't it occurred to you that I might be in love with your grandson?' Mrs. Condrycke emitted what I can best describe as a snort and inquired what love had to do with marriage. Mrs. Donald then replied, 'I'm afraid you're too advanced in your views for me, Granny,' and the episode ended with general merriment, in which the elder Mrs. Condrycke joined."

"Did she generally laugh at the jokes they seem to be so fond of around here?"

"One could never predict how Mrs. Condrycke would react. In general she appeared to enjoy other people's discomfiture."

"Do they do it all the time, or is it laid on for company?"

"The jesting is customary, sir. Squire is greatly taken with stories of the late Queen Alexandra and her royal brood engaged in innocent merriment."

"I suppose he doesn't have the scope up here to do an Edward VII."

"That, sir, is about it. So long as Squire has a regal precedent to follow, he doesn't much care who set it. On the whole, I think he also realizes the continual horseplay provides a

more or less healthy outlet for the hostilities that might otherwise become aggravated by so confined a situation."

"That's good sense. Instead of ripping somebody up the
back with a butcher knife, you put a spider in his soup.
There's a motto for the force, Madoc." Janet yawned. "Laugh
and the world laughs with you. Stab and you stab alone."

"Darling, you're barely keeping your eyes open. Come over
here on the sofa with me," Rhys coaxed. "Ludovic won't
mind if you nap a bit."

"Perhaps Miss Wadman would allow me to tuck the afghan
about her," the butler suggested gallantly.

Miss Wadman would. With her head cradled on her sweetheart's manly bosom and her nether limbs swathed in cro-
cheted wool, she dropped off to slumber as decorously as the
heroine of any Victorian novel. Ludovic surveyed the charming tableau with parental benignity.

"It is a great pity that Miss Wadman could not have paid
her visit to Graylings at a more auspicious time."

Madoc smoothed the soft bronze-brown curls away from
Janet's clear forehead. "Poor Jenny. She's not had a decent
night's sleep since we got engaged. I wish this storm would
break so we could airlift her out of here."

"She appears content to be where she is at the moment,
sir."

"Ah, she's a good little woman, my Jenny. Would you happen to know, Ludovic, whether Babs Condrycke is much of
an athlete?"

"Meaning would she at this time be capable of opening that
door against the wind, sir? I should be inclined to think not.
Last winter the family took up snowmobile racing and Mrs.
Donald took a bad spill, sustaining a fractured arm and torn
ligaments in her left shoulder. She was in a cast until Easter-
time and did therapy for some time afterward. I believe she
has still not regained total command of the arm. I noticed this
morning that she had to leave off trimming the Christmas tree
as the reaching and stretching bothered her."

"She carried all those trimmings down from the attic, though."

"Yes, sir, but only to the foot of the attic steps, which is a short flight. That appears to have been all she could manage. I believe she made some comment to that effect."

"So she did, and stuck me up on the ladder while she sent Jenny off with that Robbins chap to bring them down. A fat lot of good it did her."

Rhys snuggled his sleeping beauty with pardonable self-satisfaction. "Babs was quite right about being in a spot, you know. After all, she and Cyril were the only ones out there with Aunt Addie, and Cyril was in no shape to remember what might or might not have happened."

"You may or may not be right about their being the only ones present, sir, if I may make so bold as to contradict you. The upstairs facilities had been visited by most of the party after dinner, and it is not impossible that one of them did not return to the Great Hall. Everyone's being in costume does suggest certain possibilities, does it not?"

"Such as what?"

"For one thing, Mr. Herbert might have got one of his helpers to dress in a duplicate of that distinctive lobster costume and slip into the Great Hall in his stead for a brief time. I suppose that appears a farfetched idea."

"It's worth considering, Ludovic. Would any of the men be willing?"

"For a joke, and for an extra Christmas bonus, I should say any of them might be willing to do almost anything right now. They're all bored and fed-up at not being able to go home to their families on Christmas Eve because of the storm. Baptiste would be about the right size and build to pass for Herbert. The difficulty would be in Mr. Herbert's getting his aunt and Mr. Cyril into the hall at the same time. He could have had no way of knowing it would happen fortuitously."

"That may not have been part of the plan. Putting Aunt Addie out in the snow could have been a last-minute inspiration. A simple push down that crazy, twisting staircase would have been equally effective if Herbert's main objective was to have her wind up dead."

"But why, sir?"

"One can only conjecture. Perhaps Miss Adelaide knew her sister had been murdered and by whom. Perhaps she didn't yet know but somebody was afraid she'd find out. Did those so-called present'ments of hers ever work retroactively?"

"Often, sir. I can testify to that."

Ludovic smiled ruefully. "On occasion, we have ladies of, shall I say, susceptible tendencies staying at Graylings. It was only this past August that a comely member of her sex found occasion to remind me privately that it is more blessed to give than to receive."

"And you and she were jointly blessed, eh?" Rhys grinned. "Ludovic, you devil!"

"Those were more or less Miss Adelaide's words some weeks after the lady had departed and the light dawned. I managed to convince Miss Adelaide that I was merely upholding Squire's tradition of hospitality. At least, I think I did."

"What did Squire himself think?"

"Fortunately he was not present at the time. Miss Adelaide and I were alone."

"Was that tact or just luck?"

"Just luck, sir. Miss Adelaide was well meaning but never tactful. She would have said the same thing in front of a houseful of distinguished guests. It was her habit to blurt out whatever came into her head at any given moment regardless of the possible consequences."

"And everyone would have believed her?"

"She did have this alarming way of being right, sir."

"Yes, well, that would be reason enough to put her out of the way if you'd just killed her sister, wouldn't it? One would never know when Miss Addie might go off like a time bomb."

"Precisely, sir."

"Getting back to the notion of somebody's impersonating somebody else this evening. You do think it would have been feasible?"

"Don't you, sir? There was the diversion of the Phantom Ship, then Mr. Cyril was striving to attract everyone's attention to himself. He was standing under the kissing ball in the main doorway that leads out into the front hall, by the stairway. However, as you have doubtless observed, there are other doors, the one at the opposite end through which you helped to drag the Yule log, and a small one on the side where the fireplace is. This last door is now partially obscured by the large Christmas tree in that corner. It would not be any great feat for some member of the party to stroll around behind the tree, slip out that door, and have somebody else slip in wearing a similar costume. If the impostor remained more or less in the shadow of the tree, he could no doubt escape detection for at least a short time. You may recall that the battery lantern intended to illuminate the tree from behind had ceased to operate. It is no great trick to put a battery lantern out of commission."

"Good point, Ludovic. I can't quite buy Baptiste in a spare lobster costume, though. For one thing, he seems a bit redundant since there were already three lobsters besides Herbert. With everyone moving around, as you say, three could easily pass for four. There would also be the problem of Baptiste's getting out of that complicated arrangement of claws and feelers after he'd done his impersonation, without being caught and blowing the so-called joke. On the other hand, I can easily see Lawrence taking off that coonskin coat and porkpie hat for someone else to put on, or even Squire swapping his crimson robe and fur-trimmed cap. They'd be quick enough to exchange, and if Baptiste or whoever decided he'd better clear out he could just drop them and go. If they were found, it would be assumed the wearer had got too hot and shed his costume to give himself a breather. Where does that little door lead to?"

"Into the back passage that runs to the kitchen and the woodshed, sir. We use it mostly for bringing in wood and so forth."

"Does that passage connect with the front hallway?"

"No, but it does have a back stair leading to the second floor. One could easily go up the back way and down the front."

"One could, indeed. Do you think any one of the Condrycke men could have opened that front door single-handed under tonight's conditions?"

"I assume you are including Mr. Herbert and Mr. Lawrence, although their family name is White. They happen to be cousins. One does tend to think of them all as Condryckes, especially as there is such a strong physical resemblance. To answer your question, I should say yes. They are exceptionally powerful men. Even Squire is in remarkable shape for a man of his years. Whoever it was might have got Mr. Cyril to help, you know, and then run off leaving him holding the baby, as it were."

"Then why didn't he say so?"

"I don't know, sir. Unless Mr. Cyril thought it was himself."

"Eh?"

"Well, sir, a person could wrap a blanket around himself and stick a cap on his head; perhaps even pick up the one Mr. Cyril himself had been wearing and use that. I noticed it had fallen off in the fracas. Considering the state he was in at the time, Mr. Cyril might think he was confronting his own doppelgänger, if that is the word."

"Good God, man, you've missed your calling. You ought to be writing stories for fantastic fiction magazines."

"It's just that I've known the Condryckes so long, sir. Dressing up as each other is one of their tricks."

"I might have known it would be."

"Oh, yes. Being so much alike, they can be amazingly convincing sometimes. Year before last during the mumming they all kept changing costumes until nobody knew which was who. Even the women passed for the men and vice versa."

"Everyone laughing heartily the while, no doubt. How far does this game of Happy Families go? For instance, did the younger generation dislike Granny as much as she appears to have despised them?"

"I should say a lot of it was verbal, sir. They were used to her, you see. A good deal of resentment was expressed, but in some ways I think they were proud of her spirit. The late Mrs. Condrycke was what is known, I believe, as a conversation piece."

"One could always raise a chuckle with an account of Granny's latest tantrum, eh?"

"Something of the sort, sir."

"But were her outbursts really so terribly amusing? Didn't they ever get ticked off to the point of retaliation? This business of stealing her teeth last night, for instance. It was funny, but it was also a damned unkind thing to do, embarrassing an old woman and making her miss what might be her last chance to do something she enjoyed."

"Quite so, sir. On the other hand, the gathering would have been less merry if she had been present. Mrs. Condrycke was not improving in temper."

"Going senile, was she?"

"No, sir. Just nastier. Her mind was sharp as ever and her tongue even sharper. Not to speak ill of the dead, just giving you the facts, sir."

"So the teeth were taken as a deliberate effort to keep Granny upstairs, do you think?"

"There is often method in the Condrycke madness, sir."

"Would anybody have an opportunity to steal the teeth?"

"Anybody who was sufficiently bloody, bold, and resolute, sir. Mrs. Condrycke napped a good deal. While she was in the comparative privacy of her own suite, her teeth were apt to be kept in a glass of water on her nightstand. They did not fit so well as they once had, her gums having no doubt shrunk with age. She blamed the dentist and refused to go back to have them altered."

"Was it unusual for people to go in and out of her room without a special invitation?"

"It would be the custom rather than the exception, though of course one went through the motions of requesting admission before entering. She resented visitors' presence if they came, but complained of neglect if they stayed away. What she needed was a paid nurse-companion, but she refused to let one be hired. That would have given the family an excuse not to dance constant attendance upon her, you see."

"One begins to wonder why nobody thought to stifle Granny sooner. So in fact you had two autocrats on the premises."

"That's what it amounted to, sir."

Rhys picked up the nuance in Ludovic's tone. "And you're wondering if Squire had decided there was room for only one."

The butler performed the unbutlerian gesture of scratching his nose. "I think Squire's penchant for autocracy has been growing on him of late years, sir. Mrs. Condrycke's habit of reminding Squire that he was in fact subservient to her grace and favor did not sit well, and such reminders have been coming more and more frequently. She has also taken to thwarting Squire in a number of his projected undertakings, whereas in past years she had been content to leave most matters in his hands. For instance, she sided with Cyril against Squire's cherished plan to complete the electrification of Graylings."

"I thought someone said Cyril and Lawrence were the prime objectors."

"Mr. Lawrence is well aware of where the true power would lie. For so long as Mrs. Condrycke lived, Lawrence would have been able to come up with sound fiscal or legal reasons why her wishes should be obeyed."

"Thank you, Ludovic," said Rhys. "I have found our chat most illuminating. I am now going to deputize you, if you don't mind."

"I shall be honored, sir. What is it you wish to deputize me for?"

"The most important job there is to do here. Stay where you are and keep an eye on my Jenny. Don't wake her up. Just watch. If anybody tries to come near her with intent to harm, tear out his liver and stomp on it. That's an order."

"It shall be obeyed, sir."

Rhys eased Janet ever so gently out of his arms. She murmured fretfully in her sleep and groped for his warm presence. It was almost more than flesh could bear, but the Code of the North is a stern one. After one last, frenzied embrace, Detective Inspector Madoc Rhys went back on duty.

CHAPTER 18

Back in the library, Janet slumbered on. So, if truth be told, did Ludovic. He was not required to commit mayhem on any interloper because nobody interloped and, like Rhys, the butler had developed the knack of dropping into light but refreshing repose whenever he got the chance.

While these two enjoyed their peaceful interlude, Madoc Rhys prowled. Using his baby pocket flash and what little light there was from the ever-burning Yule log, he practiced slipping in and out of the Great Hall by the back door. He followed the service passage to a steep, uncarpeted staircase, went up it, and after one or two false turns managed to find the front stairs. Then he went back and did it again, this time pausing to imagine himself doffing a velvet robe or a coonskin coat and handing it to the confederate who would have had to stand cooling his heels until such time as an opportunity for the trick might or might not present itself.

He'd taken careful note of the time when he set off the second trip and tried to move quickly, like someone who knew the house. Even so, it was no slouch of a clamber. Furthermore, it was damned cold because he'd had to run in sock feet in order not to wake those who were, if not rapt in slumber, at least now quiescent on the second floor. He went into his own room to put on his new russet-colored pullover under his dinner jacket and to ease his frosted toes into his fleece-lined slippers. He ruined the set of the jacket by stuffing his two-way radio into the breast pocket.

The very model of a modern detective inspector, Rhys then unlocked Cyril's bedroom door and found the prisoner having a nightmare, which didn't surprise him, all things considered. He next visited the temporary mortuary where the two old sisters, Rosa and Adelaide, lay stiff and stark on the same bed. Their bodies weren't going to tell him anything he didn't know already. He borrowed the efficient battery-operated table lamp they wouldn't be needing any more and went on with his explorations.

Rhys explored for quite some time. It was well into the early hours of Christmas when he got back to the library.

"Jenny. Jenny darling, wake up. I need you."

"I need you, too, Madoc."

She nestled into his sweater front and resumed her nap. Rhys, a well-read man, remembered a piece of advice once dealt out by Bertie Wooster's infallible manservant. Jeeves had suggested the best way to capture a young woman's undivided attention was to clasp her in one's brawny arms and rain kisses on her upturned face.

As usual, Jeeves was there with the goods when needed. Janet woke. So did Ludovic, although he had the tact to pretend he hadn't until Janet was fully alert and Madoc able to get his mind back on his job.

"Jenny, listen. I need you."

"I know."

She twined her arms around his neck and raised her lips again in happy expectation.

"Not like that, love. I mean, yes like that, but not now. The thing of it is, I've found out who killed those two old women."

"Madoc! He's not chasing you with axes and throwing knives?"

"No, dearest, nobody's after me with anything. You're the only one who knows I've found out. Unless Ludovic's awake. Good morning, Ludovic."

"Good morning, sir. Merry Christmas. Are you planning an immediate arrest?"

"As to that, there's a bit of a snag. So far I haven't been able to drum up much of a case."

"So that's what you need me for, eh?" Janet disentangled herself from her beloved and shook out her skirt. She was ready for action. "It's one of the Condryckes, isn't it?"

"Oh yes. So I should think what we have to do is play a practical joke."

"Not a wiggly caterpillar like with Mad Carew?"

"No, love, not a caterpillar. Listen."

Janet listened. Then she shivered. "Ugh! Must I?"

"Not if you don't care to."

"Madoc, I didn't mean I wouldn't. I just meant—well, naturally I will if you say so. It's the only way, isn't it?"

"I don't know, Jenny. It may not work at all. It's just that my head's not working straight any more because I'm so damned fed up with Graylings, and I've got to get you out of here somehow. Ludovic, what's the best way to get them all downstairs before they've had time to think?"

"We could ring the alarm bell, sir. We are very conscious of fire danger at Graylings. Squire is wont to hold unannounced fire drills. At sound of the bell, which is in fact a loud one, everyone is required to rush to the Great Hall for a nose count, and thence to safety."

"Would the bell wake the staff?"

"Not likely, sir. Their sleeping quarters are in the cinder-block building at the far end of the barns. They have a separate battery-operated smoke alarm."

"Good. Then here's what we do."

Rhys explained. Janet and Ludovic listened, goggle-eyed.

"Now, do you two think you can manage that? It's not so difficult, you see, mostly a matter of timing."

"I just hope it will do the trick," said Janet. "Sorry. I didn't mean to talk about tricks. It's," she shivered, "not funny, is it? Anyway, I'll try."

"Good girl. Now, Ludovic, would you normally be in the house at this time of night?"

"Yes, sir. I don't sleep in the dormitory with the others. My bedroom is off the butler's pantry, near the kitchen."

"Then you'd better go put on your bathrobe and slippers in case you're spotted. No point in getting you fired if we can avoid it. In any event, you're to stay away from the Great Hall till it's all over. Your job is to sound the alarm, then hare it for the attic. Can you get there without being seen?"

"I'll use the back stairs, sir. It's faster anyway. If I should happen to meet anyone, I could say I was on my way to tell the guests what the bell was for."

"Never lie if you can help it. Just urge them to proceed with all haste. Now, how do we get the doings for Janet?"

"They are in the kitchen, sir. I put them on the warming rack pending instructions."

"Excellent. You have a bathroom out there, I suppose? With a mirror? You'll have to make do with flour or something, Jenny."

"There is talcum powder in the bathroom," said Ludovic.

"Ah, good. So long as it's not heavily scented. Then I'll go mend the fire in the Great Hall so there's just light enough to see by and make sure that bulb's still burning by the front stairs. We don't want anybody breaking his neck on the way down. Two corpses around here are plenty. Is anybody apt to charge in waving a flashlight, do you think?"

"I rather doubt it, sir. Everyone's so used to having lights left burning in the hallways, you see, and they'll still be half asleep."

"So are you, I daresay. I'm sorry to involve you in this, Ludovic."

"It is a refreshing novelty to be on the side of the law, sir. Will you step this way, Miss Wadman?"

Janet followed the butler. Rhys attended to his small chores, then prowled up and down the abominably cold Great Hall, wondering if he was out of his mind to be staging this bit of theatrics, hoping his beloved wouldn't catch pleurisy or worse out of it. At least Jenny had her thermal underwear on.

He must remember to send an official note of commendation to the manufacturer if he got her out of this in one piece.

Had he done everything he should? Rhys had several minor panics before he managed to convince himself that he'd left everything set upstairs. Now if his two amateur helpers managed to carry it off!

At least Janet looked her part. Rhys almost jumped out of his skin when she came back into the Great Hall.

"Good God! You'll do."

"Are my hands cold enough?"

"Lord, yes. I wish you could go over to the fire and warm them, but you mustn't. Stay back in the shadow of that high-boy over there and watch till I give you the signal. Now, Ludovic, ring that alarm and run like hell!"

CHAPTER 19

The fire alarm was not loud enough to wake the Graylings dead, but it roused the living fast enough. Condryckes surged down the zigzag staircase in a blond tidal wave. Some had on bathrobes, some blankets. Val was in hysterics and, again, little else. Roy had gallantly waited to put on his pajamas at whatever risk to life and limb, and was the last one down in consequence.

As Ludovic had predicted, they'd none of them thought to grab a flashlight except Herbert, and his turned out to be the kind that was really a cigar lighter so it cast little light and soon ran out of fluid.

"What's the matter?"

"Where's the fire?"

"Who rang the alarm?"

Nobody answered because nobody knew. Suspicions arose and tempers began to flare.

"If this is somebody's idea of a joke . . ."

"Herb, if those whelps of yours . . ."

Now was the moment. Rhys gave his signal. Janet glided out of her hiding place and gripped a bare wrist in her ice-cold hand.

"Hark!"

Somebody screamed. Rhys threw open the heavy plush draperies. There in the bay lay the Phantom Ship, farther away than last night but more bright, more real, more utterly terrifying.

"It's coming for you," Janet croaked. "Why did you throw me out the window?"

All the women and most of the men were screaming now. Janet clung like the grim death she was supposed to represent.

"Why did you do it? Why did you kill me?"

"Because I couldn't stand it any longer! Scraping and smiling, fawning and flattering, dancing attendance on that ghastly sister of yours so she wouldn't cut off Donald's allowance while your Goddamned nephew Herbert put fake mice down my back. Somebody should have smothered her years ago, but as usual you all left the dirty work to me. She was right. I was a fool to marry Donald. I—my God, what are you making me say?"

"You were saying that you have murdered Rosa Condrycke and Adelaide Stebbins, so it is my painful duty to arrest you, Barbara Condrycke," said Detective Inspector Rhys. "If everybody would quit screaming at once," he added plaintively, "it would be easier for me to charge the prisoner according to rules and regulations."

"I didn't do it," Babs cried.

"You just said you did."

"I was—I was joking. I was frightened! I—I thought Aunt Addie—she was here, right beside me. She had hold of me! Clara, you saw her. May? She—where did she go?"

"Back where she came from, one would think," said Rhys.

According to schedule, Janet had slipped away as soon as she'd startled Babs into confessing, got behind the Christmas tree, and rushed from the Great Hall, with Ludovic running interference for her in a dark brown robe that had made him almost invisible among the crowd. She ought to be in the butler's private bathroom any second now, washing the talcum powder off her face and changing out of Aunt Addie's cold, wet clothes.

He wasn't about to explain all that even if he could have made himself heard above this fearful racket. He'd had an easier time of it charging Mad Carew. Then it had been only himself, the maniac, and a fuzzy caterpillar.

"Babs, you couldn't!" May was wailing. "Babs, you wouldn't do that!"

"She could, she would, and she did," Rhys answered for his captive. "What defeated her was the dim light. Babs didn't see the little fold of curtain she'd left pinched in the window."

"What window?" Lawrence demanded.

"The one on the third landing of the front staircase, which is directly over the front door and for some reason does not have a storm window fastened over it like the rest of the windows in the house. You did not have to go through that elaborate business of proving your sister-in-law could not have opened the door in the storm. Babs knew she couldn't, so she never tried. It took very little strength to raise the window, though she might have been more careful not to leave her fingerprints on the glass. I assume they are hers because they match the ones I found on the projector in the attic."

"Projector? You mean a slide projector?" yelped Herbert. "You're crazy. We don't have one. How could we?"

"Ah, but you do. How do you think the Phantom Ship has managed to time its appearances so neatly during recent years? Mrs. Babs acquired a color transparency, perhaps by coating a ship model with phosphorus and setting it afire against a dark background so that it would blend into the darkness outside, you see, and blaze up with a fine dramatic effect. I suppose she planned the stunt originally as her private joke against her in-laws."

"Yes, but how?" Herbert insisted.

"She is an ingenious lady. She rigged up a projector on a little turntable, and activated it by a contrivance involving a kitchen timer, a battery like the ones you use in your big lanterns, and a large elastic band. The timer was rigged to switch on the projector and release the turntable together, so that the ship would appear to be sailing up the bay. It was set to stay on only a few seconds so you'd have time for only a quick glimpse when the image showed up against those big rocks near the shore. I suppose none of you ever thought of a slide projector because, as Herbert says, how could you have one here?"

"But if it was just a trick, how did Aunt Addie always know?" said Clara.

"That, I cannot tell you. One would doubt she and Babs planned the joke between them because, as everyone keeps telling me, Aunt Addie was inclined to blurt out whatever came into her head. Perhaps Babs always had a certain air of expectancy about her after she had sneaked up to set the timer and knew the ship was due to appear at a certain moment. Aunt Addie may have come to recognize that as a signal without realizing she did so. She was, I should say, a simple-minded woman. People with so-called psychic abilities often are, I believe. They don't have intricate thought processes of their own to get in the way of the vibrations, you see."

"Poppycock!" shouted Donald. "You can't prove my wife killed anybody."

"You heard her say she did. There are also the fingerprints that will turn out to be hers. There is the fact that your wife, despite a supposedly weak arm, managed to lug an immense number of boxes down from the attic yesterday morning rather than allow anyone else to go up there and happen to discover her projector. She'd had to leave it set up, you see, because it's rather a tricky thing to adjust and she knew she wouldn't have time last night because of the mumming and so forth. Having killed Rosa, she needed the ghost ship again to set the stage for Aunt Addie's murder. It is interesting to note that Miss Adelaide sensed she was intended to die last evening. She told Miss Wadman so, although she did not appear to know how or at what time it would happen."

"That brings up a nice point," Lawrence broke in. "Would you care to tell us precisely how Babs was supposed to know when Aunt Addie would be leaving the Great Hall with Cyril?"

"I don't expect it mattered one way or another. I should suppose Babs originally planned to smother Aunt Addie in her sleep, that method having worked so well with Granny the previous evening. Pushing Miss Adelaide out the window to freeze and throwing the blame on Cyril was probably an inspiration of the moment. Being the wife of a man like Donald, Babs has no doubt had plenty of practice at snatching a favorable opening. The sooner she got Aunt Addie out of the way, the better for her, of course. She must have been sweating all evening. The old lady's reputation for infallibility was so well entrenched, you see, and she had been running on a good deal about Rosa."

Rhys noticed that Janet, now clad from head to toe in blue fleece, had entered the Great Hall, still guarded by Ludovic in brown Jaeger. He swallowed, for his throat was dry and he still couldn't believe this ridiculous stunt had come off.

"There is also the interesting fact that Miss Adelaide Stebbins appears to have been a well-to-do woman in her own right and has left her entire estate to Donald. The will is in her handkerchief case, along with a note explaining that she didn't mean to slight the rest of you but she felt Donald had been unfairly treated when his grandfather left everything to Cyril simply because he happened to have been born first, and she wanted to redress the wrong insofar as her means allowed."

"But I didn't know that," Donald protested.

"I'm not saying you did. It would be a woman and not a man whom a maiden lady of Miss Adelaide's generation would let go prowling through her bureau drawers. Mrs. Babs spoke feelingly a moment ago about being the one to get all the dirty work, and I've noticed myself that she seemed to take on various little chores more or less as if they were expected of her. I'm sure she's been called upon to nurse your great-aunt through certain of the ills to which elderly flesh is heir or as in this case, heiress."

"That's right," said Clara, ever the soul of charity. "You have, Babs. You even made a special trip up here to nurse Aunt Addie after she had her gallstones out."

"That proves nothing!"

"The bits of dark green fuzz from that mohair pullover you had on the night Granny died prove something, however," said Rhys. "You left some on the rug in her room. Was that when you killed her, or earlier when you stole her teeth to provide a reason why she couldn't come down?"

"I did not steal those disgusting teeth. Aunt Addie did that herself, if you want to know. She told me so. Old Rosa had been in such a foul mood all day that Addie thought she'd do the family a favor and keep her sister upstairs."

"A very good story, Mrs. Babs, as I'm sure Lawrence will agree. You are endeavoring to establish a nice distinction between premeditated and unpremeditated murder, are you?"

"I am merely telling the truth, Inspector Rhys. I'm not surprised you don't recognize it when you hear it. As to the fuzz from my sweater, what if I did shed some in Granny's room? I went in to say hello to her after we'd got here, naturally. So did the others. She'd have thrown a tantrum if we hadn't. I'm sure I had on the green sweater then because I'd changed the moment I got here. That's the warmest outfit I own. You can't hang me for trying to keep from freezing, can you?"

"I can't hang you for anything," Rhys answered gently and sadly. "There is no death penalty in Canada, as you doubtless know. Anyway, sentencing is up to the judge. I found another bit of that same green fuzz caught in the projector, which has already been impounded as evidence in case anybody has the bright idea of sneaking upstairs to smash it," he added with a glance at Roy.

"Again, it must have been the handicap of having to operate in a bad light that did you in, since you are such a clever lady. You were being clever when you pointed out in front of us all that you were counting on me to get you clear. What you meant was that you were counting on my being too stupid to see through your colossal bluff. You thought nobody could believe a nice woman like you would have the brass to do what you did. You would be surprised to learn how many other nice women have made the same mistake."

CHAPTER 20

May had been weeping, not silently, into the lining of her father's fur and velvet cap. She gave one last, mighty sniff and was about to wipe her nose on the cap when she realized what she was holding and used one of her extraneous lobster legs instead.

"Where's Aunt Addie? I told you she'd come to. I knew we should have kept on with the hot-water bottles."

"May, you're dreaming," said Clara.

"I am not! I saw her. She grabbed Babs and asked why she threw her out the window. I heard her myself. Where is she now? Answer me that!"

"Whatever you saw was not Aunt Addie," Rhys answered with perfect truth. "Miss Adelaide is lying dead on your grandmother's bed upstairs, where your husband carried her after Mrs. Donald Condrycke smothered her in the curtain and pushed her out the staircase window."

"I did not!" Babs screamed. "None of this is true. I told you I passed Cyril and Aunt Addie downstairs in the front hall. She was an old woman. She moved slowly."

"She had been skipping through the house like a young lamb during the mumming," Rhys contradicted. "I do not believe you passed her. I believe you caught up with her, ascended with her to that conveniently placed window and probably made some remark like, 'Let's look out and see if the snow has stopped.'

"It had not, so you went ahead with your plan. You stifled her with folds of the curtain, which is of heavy plush like all the curtains at Graylings. You shoved her either dead or unconscious out the window, counting on the heavily falling snow to eradicate the mark her body made sliding over the sill. You did not have to be gentle with Aunt Addie as you had with Granny, you see, because any bruises on her body would be blamed on Cyril's attacking her."

"Which he did. This is absurd, Inspector Rhys. If I'd met Aunt Addie on the stairs, I'd have met Cyril, too. How could I commit a murder with him looking on?"

"You could not, of course, so I should say you must have sent him back to the front hall by a ruse. You probably told him my—Miss Wadman had changed her mind and was waiting for him under the mistletoe," snarled the Mountie.

"As soon as you'd disposed of Miss Adelaide, you ran back to Cyril and forced him over against the front door. You staged your struggle quite effectively, but the poor, muddled chap was in fact trying to fend you off rather than to attack you when you began screaming for help and rounding up your witnesses. His managing to get in a whack with the cane was all to the good, as far as you were concerned. Otherwise, you'd have had to fake up some injuries yourself."

"That's terribly clever, Inspector. If I was attacking Cyril instead of the other way round, why didn't he say so?"

"I was wondering that myself, until I had a chance to look him over thoroughly. You managed to give him a jab of something or other during the melee, knowing the amphetamines you'd slipped into his drink to make him act crazy would also tend to keep him awake and restless. You made a dreadfully clumsy job if it. He's got a hematoma the size of Prince Edward Island on his hip. That's why he folded so abruptly, as those who had to drag him upstairs will testify. God knows what sort of shape the poor chap will be in when he wakes up."

"He'd damn well better wake up," shouted Herbert. "Hell, I like old Cy. Babs," he delivered the Condryckes' most shattering condemnation, "that wasn't funny."

"My son!"

Squire had at last made up his mind which role to play. "The heir to Graylings."

"Yes, well, Cyril might not have been the heir much longer," said Rhys. "I'm sure Mrs. Babs had her husband's interests at heart. Cyril might have spent the rest of his life in a prison for the criminally insane, but I think it more likely he would soon be found dead. Eaten by remorse for his foul attack on Aunt Adelaide, he would have committed suicide and sewn the whole package up very neatly. The suicide would have to wait until he'd worked the drugs out of his system, so that an autopsy would not reveal anything so amiss as it would right now."

"And where am I supposed to have gotten all these drugs I don't even know the names of?" Babs was still fighting.

"I cannot believe that, traveling in fashionable circles as you do, you have never come upon somebody who could give you that information." Rhys's gentle dark eyes rested momentarily on Val. "By the way, you may be interested to know that it quit snowing rather abruptly a little while ago. The marks on the windowsill up there are still quite easily discernible. You might as well come quietly, you know."

Babs looked around her, at all those other big, blond people. She was no longer one of them. She had broken the rules, and out she must go. Even her own daughter wouldn't meet her eyes. As for her husband; he had, after all, been trained always to side with the majority.

"Yes, Babs," said Donald in the same calm, cool tone he might have used to a hostile member of the board, "you might as well go quietly."

CHAPTER 21

"Val wanted to be on television," said Janet. "I daresay she'll get her chance now."

Using his miniature radio, Madoc had sent for help, and got it. A photographer, a fingerprint expert, and most importantly a policewoman to take charge of Babs Condrycke had been flown in within the hour. There'd been more investigating, more taking of statements, much snapping of pictures. The slide projector with its ghostly transparency was taken away as evidence. So were the pillow from Granny's bed and the curtain from the stairway window. So also was Cyril, though they had a terrible problem rousing him enough to travel.

Even on Christmas, a cortège containing two corpses, a man so befuddled he could hardly stand up, a group of RCMP personnel, a stony-faced society woman in handcuffs, along with her husband, daughter, family lawyer, and a much agitated young chap who was vaguely described as a friend of the family could hardly fail to attract notice.

However, the press photographers failed to observe and perhaps wouldn't have believed that the diffident little man trailing along at the rear happened to be the legendary captor of Mad Carew; and that the charming though equally modest little woman clinging to his arm was the affianced bride of Detective Inspector Rhys. Madoc and his Jenny contrived to slip away without landing in the headlines along with the rest. Still, it had been an awkward business.

Less awkward than the departure from Graylings, to be

sure. Taking leave of a host whose hospitality had been lavish and whose daughter-in-law one had got arrested for murder required a brand of etiquette that not even Lady Rhys would have managed comfortably.

There were, naturally, any number of royal precedents for bumping off one's kith and kin with an eye to the main chance. Still, any such remark as, "Cheer up, Squire. Chances are Eleanor of Aquitaine would have done the same," seemed hardly the thing.

Janet had decided their most tactful course would be simply to pack their bags and go away. Madoc could not have agreed more, though he did tell Ludovic on the QT to look them up in Fredericton if he got fired for testifying to having overheard Mrs. Donald's confession.

Babs Condrycke, handcuffed to a policewoman as she was, had also realized she might as well heed the family's advice and leave quietly. She'd begun to take the line that Madoc Rhys was an arrogant young booby trading on his connections and playing at cops and robbers like some provincial Lord Peter Wimsey, that Granny had died a natural death as a result of overindulgence in wassail, that Aunt Addie had committed suicide by hurling herself from the window while of unsound mind, having always been shaky in the intellect as everybody knew, and that Lawrence had better get her the best defense lawyer in Canada not because she needed one but because the honor of Graylings was at stake.

Mrs. Donald Condrycke would get her lawyer, of course, because she was quite right about the honor of Graylings, and Lawrence would have briefed the top man in any case. She might even get a jury to swallow her story. The policewoman had allowed her prisoner to change into traveling clothes. Babs looked so elegant in her mink coat and hat that Rhys thought it entirely possible she could breeze through to an acquittal on sheer force of personality. A few years from now she might be entertaining dinner parties with an amusing account of her ridiculous misunderstanding with the RCMP. Then again she mightn't.

Madoc and his Jenny had at last managed to escape from Fredericton headquarters, all notes typed up, all depositions filed, all evidence tagged, all jokes about matrimony from envious colleagues patiently borne. They'd retrieved his unglamorous car from the parking lot where he'd left it when they'd set off on that fateful ride in the helicopter, put in the battery his kind fellow officers had been keeping warm for him back at the shop, and got started easily enough.

As he turned out of the lot, Janet remarked, "Well, Val wanted to be on television."

Madoc nodded. "I expect Miss Val will get her innings on the news tonight, but let's forget her and the whole blasted business for the moment. Jenny, I'm scared to ask this, but I have to. Now that you've found out what sort of thing you'd be getting yourself in for, do you still want to marry me?"

To his astonishment, Janet burst out laughing. "Want to? Madoc, you darling idiot, there's no way I could get out of it. Can't you imagine the talk there'll be in Pitcherville tonight? They all know I've been at Graylings with you. The party line will be blazing hot five seconds after the news comes on. I only wish we could manage the wedding right this instant, while I may just possibly still have a few shreds of reputation left."

"Let's see. We might have ourselves dropped by parachute to a ship in midocean and get the captain to oblige. That does seem a bit complicated. Besides, I'd hate to have you too seasick to say I do. You do, Jenny darling, don't you? I mean, Pitcherville notwithstanding?"

Janet managed with no trouble at all to convince him that she really, truly, honest-to-goodness did. Madoc then had the bright idea of hunting up the police chaplain with results eminently satisfactory to himself, Janet, the chaplain who was flattered to be asked, and the chaplain's wife who thought they made a lovely couple and wouldn't they stay for Christmas high tea?

They said thanks but they wouldn't. By then both were half-starved and wholly exhausted, but what they needed more than food or rest was a chance to be alone together. Madoc's drab little bachelor apartment didn't promise anything more than a packet of tea, a few stale buns, and a lumpy single bed; but it was a place to go, so they went.

"I'd carry you over the threshold, Jenny love, but I'll have to park the suitcases first."

"Never mind me. After what you've been through, you'll do well to carry yourself."

"Oh, I'm not all that worn out."

Madoc made rather a business of helping Janet out of her jacket. She was warm, she was sweet, she was his. She was still wearing her thermal underwear. After a long, long, time he said huskily, "Jenny, what do you want to do now?"

Janet's own voice was none too firm, but she had her answer ready.

"Darling, remember last night when we got dressed up for the mumming? I said I didn't know what I was supposed to represent, and you said I was your Christmas present?"

He kissed the tip of her nose, his dark eyes now far from wistful. "Yes love, I remember. And so?"

"Well, my goodness," she whispered. "It's Christmas, isn't it? Aren't you going to unwrap your present?"

Alisa Craig was born in New Brunswick, Canada, where *Murder Goes Mumming* is set. She is the author of two previous novels, *A Pint of Murder* and *The Grub-and-Stakers Move a Mountain.*